A Slave to His Kiss

A Slave to His Kiss

Anastasia Dubois

X
LIBRIS

An *X Libris* Book

First published by X Libris in 1995

Copyright © Anastasia Dubois 1995

The moral right of the author has been asserted

A CIP catalogue for this book
is available from the British Library

ISBN 0 7515 1344 X

Photoset in North Wales by
Derek Doyle & Associates, Mold, Clwyd
Printed and bound in Great Britain by
Clays Ltd, St Ives plc

X Libris
A Division of
Little, Brown and Company (UK)
Brettenham House
Lancaster Place
London WC2E 7EN

A Slave to His Kiss

Prologue

DEAR VENETIA, YOU just wouldn't believe how much fun I'm having down here in the South of France . . .

Cassie Fellowes rocked back on her chair, running the end of the pen through her long, wavy blonde hair. Her chin uptilted, she looked up at the ceiling fan, droning like a lazy bumble-bee as it turned round and round above her, casting shadows on the walls.

The cooling breeze from the fan was a godsend on this still, rather oppressive spring night in southern France. But then, you'd expect a wealthy and sophisticated man like Bastien le Rocq to own a villa with air-conditioning, and he hadn't disappointed her. The Villa Le Rocq boasted a swimming-pool, stables, exotic gardens, luxury bathrooms and even a master bedroom with a heart-shaped bed and mirrors on the ceiling: in fact, it had been quite a stroke of luck meeting Bastien.

When he'd invited her to spend a few days at his villa, high above the Baie des Anges, well . . . how could a girl refuse, especially when Bastien was not only drop-dead gorgeous, but utterly charming into the bargain?

Laughing to herself, Cassie tried to concentrate on the letter to Venetia. She knew she didn't write often enough to her twin sister, but Venetia was so different and after Cambridge they'd just drifted apart, gone their separate ways.

Whereas Cassie was flirty, flighty and had permanent wanderlust, Venetia was seriously into her career. Cassie thought she might want to be a writer one day, when she'd lived a little; Venetia was already a trained archeologist, working on some dreary old dig in Istanbul.

Venetia, a wage-slave already, at twenty-five. How perfectly appalling. Well, Cassie wasn't going to fall into *that* trap, no matter how many times Venetia tried to persuade her to 'settle down' and 'get a life'. That was why she'd decided to spend six months hitching around Europe before moving on to North America. Well, that, and the prospect of meeting a wealthy lover or two . . .

Having such a great time, sis – you should come and see me. I've met this truly amazing guy, and guess what! I'm staying at his villa for a day or two. I'm sure he wouldn't mind you staying here too . . .

As long as you were happy to share his bed, thought Cassie to herself with a silent chuckle. Three in a bed . . . now that was a diverting thought. When it came to sexual experimentation, Cassie thought she had tried just about everything, but surprisingly Bastien had already taught her a few bedtime games she'd never encountered before. Maybe that was what Venetia needed – more adventurous sex, to relax her a bit.

The village is pretty, and quite remote, even though it's so near Nice and the Riviera. But there are some real hunks here – you should come and join me, you really should. Get some leave and come and stay for a while. I'll show you the sights, introduce you to a few guys. What you need is bit more fun.

Fun. She'd certainly had plenty of that since she arrived in the little Riviera village of Valazur. There was Bastien, the young and handsome playboy, and Jean-Marc, the distinguished owner of a local vineyard. And then there was Esteban . . . but Esteban wasn't really her type, was he? There was something indefinable, something . . . dangerous about Esteban. No, not Esteban. There were plenty of good-looking guys to screw in Valazur, and as poor, dear, possessive Bastien

3

was so fond of saying, Esteban was a nobody. So why was it so hard to get his dark eyes out of her mind?

She glanced at the clock. Almost midnight. She could hear a hot night-wind rustling the trees outside her window, the sound of cigales singing in the darkness. Even in spring there was a tropical languour to this place, a feeling of lazy sensuality which exited her senses and aroused every nerve-ending in her body.

'Cassie . . .'

She looked up as she heard her name, whispered on the wind. Or had she heard it? Had it been nothing more than the breeze rustling in the trees, tapping their branches against the window?

Standing up, she looked out of the window into the garden. But the little pool of light cast from her window illuminated only a patch of soft green grass set amid olive trees. There was no one to be seen.

'Cassie!'

This time the voice was quite distinct, but still there was no sign of anyone underneath the window. She opened it and leaned out.

'Qui est-ce? Bastien, c'est toi? Luc? Jean-Marc?'

There was no reply. But as she drew back into the room, convinced that one of her several lovers must be playing tricks on her, she heard it again; a shivering, caressing whisper this time, so

4

compelling that on impulse she slipped on her robe and went downstairs.

The ground floor of the house was in darkness, but there was a moon tonight and the hallway was flooded with a pale, pearly luminescence. She opened the front door and walked out, barefoot, into the gardens.

It was a beautiful night, the air warm as a tropical sea, the distant scent of the ocean a spicy, salty tang. The scents of citrus and wild thyme and mimosa wafted around her, delighting her senses, making her think of tomorrow night when Bastien would return from his business trip and she would share his bed again . . .

'Cassie.'

The voice was so close that she wheeled round, certain of confronting the practical joker. But she saw nothing, for something dark and soft wrapped itself around her face, blinding her, and then there was a hand over her mouth, half-suffocating her, stopping her screams.

And then there was nothing at all. Only darkness.

Chapter One

'*MY DARLING VENETIA*, you have the most beautiful breasts I have ever seen. Do you know that, my sweet?'

Venetia Fellowes gave a low growl of pleasure as her lover Ramon knelt over her, licking the very tips of her rose-pink nipples.

'Your skin is so white and soft . . . so many English women spoil their beauty by baring their breasts to the sun. But you, my dear Venetia, you have the skin of a goddess . . .'

A half-smile of pleasure played at the corners of Venetia's mouth as her body responded instinctively to Ramon's practised caresses. She was under no illusions about Ramon's blandishments – oh, she might be attractive, with her long blonde hair and full breasts, but a goddess? Hardly. Not that it seemed to matter, not tonight. When Ramon made passionate love to her, all through the night, she could almost believe the words he whispered to her in the darkness.

A small Calor gas lamp hissed on an upturned wooden crate, which had been set beside the bed as an improvised table. Dancing shadows played all around in the eerie orange glow, illuminating a small fold-up table, typewriter, boxes of artefacts and half-open suitcase. The bed itself consisted of little more than an old mattress, topped with a pile of rough blankets.

Well, you couldn't expect luxuries when you were working for the Anglo-Turkish Archaeological Council, besides which Venetia was a very junior archaeologist. She had been lucky to get this much privacy – some of the student workers were sharing six to a tent. She thought back to Cassie's last scribbled postcard. It sounded as if her twin sister had fallen on her feet – as usual. Luxury villas, hints about millionaire lovers . . . it made quite a contrast to Venetia's spartan existence, helping to excavate recently discovered mosaic floors in a long-buried brothel outside Istanbul.

If only she didn't keep having these weird and disturbing dreams about Cassie – dreams in which nothing made sense, which were at once frightening and deeply, irresistibly sensual.

Perhaps it was the power of her own subconscious, some long-sublimated desire to be more like Cassie, to enjoy the same sexual liberation, the same unembarrassed joy in acts of pure, self-indulgent pleasure. Acts she was beginning to discover and explore with Ramon . . .

Yes, there were some advantages to being here, in this small tent, in the middle of nowhere, thought Venetia to herself as Ramon's fingers lightly caressed her naked flank.

'Mmm, yes, that feels so good,' she murmured, as his lips followed the line traced by his fingertips, garlanding her bare skin with tiny kisses.

'I know how to give you pleasure, my sweet,' smiled Ramon, his kisses moving over her belly, down, down towards the burning heart of her hungry sex.

She felt for his hand, tried to move it down towards her pubis, but he gently disengaged her grasp.

'Patience. Patience, *amore*. First, there is so much I want to do with you, to you . . . now, tell me this does not feel like paradise?'

He nipped the taut flesh of her belly, very gently, between his teeth, and Venetia squirmed with sudden and unexpected pleasure.

'Ramon! What are your doing . . .?'

He silenced her with a sudden kiss, full on the lips. A kiss which stifled all her protests. Her back

9

arched as her body surrendered to the pleasure of his touch, his embrace. Her full breasts pushed against his chest, the nipples long and hard as brazil-nuts, betraying the depth of her arousal. It had been a long time, too long by far, since any man had made her feel quite like this.

Ramon was lying on top of her now, one hand moving lightly over her skin whilst the other caressed the long, silky mane of her hair, taking out the pins and releasing it from the oh-so-practical French pleat she wore it in while she was working.

'There, my darling. You look so much more beautiful now,' he assured her. 'Once again you are my true goddess. Only I see you as you really are.'

He ran his fingers through her hair, untangling the knots, spreading it out in wild, golden waves across the pillow. He buried his face in its softness, breathing in its fragrance, running the soft strands over his skin, and she felt his manhood twitch and jerk against her belly. She could smell his arousal – the irresistibly exciting melange of sweat and semen; the salty tang of the clear juice which oozed from his glans, making damp, slippery patches on her belly.

Venetia let her hands curl loosely around him, smoothing over his bare, tanned back; feeling for the sprinkling of tiny dark hairs at the base of his spine and teasing them, pushing and stroking them the wrong way so that a shiver of excitement passed right through his body.

'*Amore, amore!*' he gasped, kissing her more passionately than ever, his fingers convulsively clutching at strands of her hair, winding and twisting them; his lips possessing her with an almost frightening hunger.

She was learning fast. If the dig lasted the full six months, by the time she returned to her dull job at the museum in London, she would have learned a very great deal about the arts of love from Ramon Jerez.

Her right leg slid over his thigh and wrapped itself around his back, the side of her foot sliding over the bare skin, caressing, seducing. She knew what she wanted, and so did Ramon. But he wanted to make it last.

'Please, Ramon, I want you.'

'Soon, my darling.'

'Please. Now. I want you now.'

He gave a throaty chuckle.

'My impetuous one, such impatience there is in you. So I must be strong for both of us. Trust me, and I will make you feel such pleasures as you have never known . . .'

Venetia let out a groan of frustrated lust as he began caressing her again, this time turning his attentions once more to her breasts. How long had they been lying here, in Venetia's tent, their naked bodies entwined? It felt like forever, as though

11

there had never been a time when she was not on the very edge of ecstasy, kept there by Ramon's wickedly skilful fingers and tongue. And he hadn't even touched her between her thighs, not yet. How long ... how long before his fingertips lighted on the burning heart of her desire?

She let out a little low moan as Ramon took her nipple between his lips, sucking it into his mouth as an infant might do, hungry for his mother's milk.

It felt so good. Ramon's fingers were gripping her breast at its base, making it swell into a generous globe, making the fine, bluish veins stand out against the nacreous flesh and the areola swell and pucker. Her nipple was unbelievably hard and almost unbearably sensitive. Each new kiss, each new flick of Ramon's tongue felt so powerful that it was as if there were power-lines all over her body, leading from the nerve-endings in her nipple to arms, and thighs, and toes and ... most unbearably of all ... to her clitoris.

The poor, neglected flower-stalk of her clit throbbed and strained between her labia, hidden by the coral-pink folds, trying desperately to push its pearly head towards the light, towards the source of intimate kisses and caresses. Venetia could feel it, its fleshy hood pushed back, its tip bare, pressing against her inner labia as she pressed her thighs together, trying desperately to bring herself to the crisis of pleasure she craved.

'You are a very bad, wicked girl,' murmured Ramon, letting go of her nipple for a moment. She looked down at it and saw how it glistened, dripping wet with rivulets of his saliva. And he slid his thigh between hers, pushing apart her legs, rubbing his thigh very gently against the hardness of her pubis.

'Oh! Oh please, harder, I can't bear it!'

But Ramon just went on teasing her, his hard-muscled thigh hardly more than brushing the tangle of her golden pubic hair, refusing the brutal caress of flesh on flesh for which her clitoris so yearned. She tried to push herself up, bring her pubis against his upper thigh, force him to make love to her the way she wanted him to; but his strength was so much greater than hers, and she was completely at the mercy of his own, tyrannical passion.

His lips sucked hard on her nipple, drawing it out into a painfully erect cone of puckered, rubbery flesh. His tongue flicked across it like a snake's, darting out, lightly teasing the very tip, sending tiny electric shocks of tingling pleasure through her famished body. With each new kiss there was some new variant of sensation, no two flicks of the tongue quite producing the same reaction.

And then he began to bite her nipples, at first with the utmost gentleness, and then with a carefully calculated brutality which took her to the limits of discomfort and then, in that split second before discomfort turns to pain, transforming the sensation into one of purest, most lascivious pleasure.

'Give it to me, oh Ramon, give it to me *hard*.' She scarcely recognised herself as the ordinary, slightly staid girl who had once been so scandalised by Cassie's sexual precociousness. At fifteen, when Venetia had still been besotted with horses and gymkhanas, Cassie had begun a steamy affair with their riding master. By nineteen, Cassie had seduced all her Cambridge supervisors. It was difficult to believe that Venetia was, at last, beginning to have adventures of her own.

Ramon's left hand was squeezing and teasing her right breast, his mouth and right hand tormenting the other, squashing the flesh into a fat white globe, biting and sucking and licking the nipple into such a crescendo of excitement that Venetia half thought she might come, without him ever having touched her swollen clit.

Just when she thought the pleasures would never end, Ramon took his mouth from her nipple and drew away.

'Oh please . . . don't stop.' Her eyes burned with yearning, pleading as she gazed up at him, drinking in the fire in his own dark eyes.

'I think it is time now for you to pleasure me, Venetia.'

He slid up her body until he was kneeling astride her breasts, his stiff manhood hanging like a curving sabre, its glistening purple tip pointing towards her moist and willing lips.

She reached up and caressed him, and he responded instantly, his body tensing with enjoyment as her cool, white fingers began stroking his balls. They were really beautiful, thought Venetia to herself – far more beautiful than she had realised before. Two heavy testes hung in their seed-purse of softly puckered skin, covered with a curling mass of wiry, dark hairs. As she touched them she felt them move within the loose bag, and it seemed to contract and grow taut at her caress, tighter and more firm.

Such beautiful treasures were too tempting not to kiss, and she put out her tongue to lick them.

'Come closer,' she begged Ramon. 'Closer, so I can kiss you properly.'

He needed no second bidding, lowering himself a little more so that his testes were actually touching her lips. Experienced as he was, Ramon could not have imagined the excitement of what happened next. For, surprising even herself, Venetia parted her lips and drew his right testicle right inside her mouth.

As her mouth closed tightly around it, she felt Ramon shiver with need, and he began to moan, his lips forming wordless sounds of desperate need.

Venetia could only guess how good it felt for Ramon to have his balls licked and sucked. She tried to imagine how it must feel to have that most intimate, that most fragile and delicate part imprisoned within a woman's mouth. How desperately arousing it must be to have the physical pleasure of her caresses, mingled with the erotic fear, the sheer vulnerability, the need to trust the lover completely and without reservation as she closes her lips about you, drawing you in, engulfing you.

'Oh . . . oh Venetia . . . oh *yes*.'

She wished so much that she could take both of his balls into her mouth at the same time. Even the thought of it turned her on so desperately that she could feel her sex-muscles lightly clenching and unclenching in the anticipation of an orgasm which seemed like some faraway dream, a fantastical impossibility which could surely never turn into reality.

She took Ramon's left testicle between her lips and began sucking it, not so hard as to cause him any real discomfort, but hard enough to give him the frisson of fear which she knew would drive him crazy with the need to spurt.

'Venetia . . . oh Venetia, you have to let me come inside you right now. I want you so much, I need to have you. I need to fuck you, I need to fuck you right now, don't you understand?'

He moved to pull out from between her lips,

but she refused him with gentle insistence. No, her eyes smiled, filled with the exhilaration of power. No, I shan't let you go, I shan't let you have what you say you want. Because it isn't what you want really, is it? What you want is for me to go on sucking your balls until you think you can't go on any longer, and then suck you some more. And when I've finished, if you're incredibly lucky, maybe I'll take your dick into my mouth . . .

Venetia was right, of course. She knew it. She could read it in Ramon's expression, in his convulsive caresses, his hoarse and heavy breathing, his hardened prick, dancing its desire as it pressed against her face, trickling its clear, salty juice over her skin.

And what a beautiful prick it was. She simply had to taste it. Parting her lips a little way, she let Ramon's testis slide, very slowly, out of her mouth. It was wet with saliva and very, very firm and full within its soft, wet purse.

At this, Ramon gave a whimper of loss; but then he realised what Venetia was going to do next.

'Do it to me. That's right, my English vixen. Take it right inside your mouth, suck on it really hard. Oh, sweet Venetia . . .'

Ramon's body was beautiful, there was no denying that. Labouring kept him gloriously fit, and all that digging on the site had hardened his muscles to steel wires beneath his deeply tanned skin. But nothing about him was quite as beautiful as his penis. It was smoothly curved, a sabre of pink flesh, swollen on the underside with knots of bulging veins which pulsed to the touch. His cock was circumcised, and the exposed glans was a rich, dark purple, glassy-smooth with the sex-juice which oozed from its single, tiny eye.

She took him between her lips and he filled her mouth with his swollen manhood, his whole shaft sliding eagerly into her, so that the glans pushed against the back of her throat and for a moment she thought she would choke. But in the next second he drew back and began thrusting, surprisingly gently, into her, his own wetness joining with the wetness of her saliva, lubricating the stiff shaft as it slid in and out of her pursed lips.

With fingers and thumb she gripped the base of his cock, squeezing quite tightly, the remainder of her fingers cupping the heavy sacs of his balls. He groaned, all restraint gone now, murmuring soft words in his own language, utterly lost in the desperate pleasure of this beautiful mouth-fuck.

Venetia wanted him to come now, wanted to make him spurt on to her tongue, to feel the power of her own sexuality as he poured a creamy tide of semen into her greedy mouth. Oh how she longed to swallow it down, so abundant that she could scarcely contain it all within her lips, swallowing hard but deliberately letting a few tiny trickles escape from her lips and run down her chin and throat.

Ramon moved slowly inside her, keeping the measure of their rhythm, refusing to let go and simply rush those last, delicious strokes towards orgasm. Venetia could feel how much his restraint was costing him, how difficult it must be not to abandon himself to the ease of instant pleasure, instead forcing himself to make it go on, and on, and on.

This was the first time she had given Ramon oral sex, and she was astonished at just how much it was turning her on. What an incredible power-high it gave her to know that she, and she alone, held the reins of his pleasure. He might be holding back, making it last, but he wasn't in control, not any longer. If Venetia chose she could bring him off with a single flick of her tongue, a single squeeze of his shaft between her fingers. His pleasure was hers too; and her own pleasure was building up, growing with every second.

When he came, it was as though the whole world were spinning upside down, the flickering lights and shadows swimming in and out of focus, nothing making any sense as the dizziness of pure ecstasy overtook them.

For Venetia, it was the ecstasy of sexual power; for Ramon, the apotheosis of physical satisfaction. As his semen jetted out of him, he felt as thought his entire soul were gushing out, pouring itself into Venetia in an opalescent tidal wave.

She swallowed it down eagerly, her thirst for him unquenched and unquenchable. She wanted more, more, more. And even as the last drops of semen lay on her tongue, she yearned for their acts of passion to begin all over again.

Ramon slid down the bed until he was lying beside her, his thigh laid across her body, rubbing lightly up and down, making her feel so horny that she thought she would die. His fingers toyed with her breasts, making her groan with hunger. Now it was Ramon who had the power and she knew it, submitting joyfully to her sensual master.

'They say Englishwomen are cold,' he smiled, watching her eyes close in mute ecstasy as he pinched her nipple between finger and thumb. 'They say they have no passion. But I know the truth, don't I, my darling?'

She moaned at his touch, her backside wriggling on the rough blanket, her buttocks parting so that the coarse woollen fabric teased the sensitive membranes within.

'Oh Ramon, don't leave me like this, please, I have to come, I have to!'

'There is no need for such impatience, Venetia. You know I can make it last. Why be in such a hurry? It will be over soon enough, and then it will be another day . . . another long day before I can be in your bed again.'

His fingers stroked her belly; long, smooth caresses, light and playful, teasing pleasure from flesh that was already tingling with delicious anticipation.

'I think I shall play with your clitoris, Venetia. Do you think you would like that?'

'Ramon, don't tease me!' Her hands scrabbled at the blanket, seeking comfort, release from the tormenting sensations boiling and bubbling inside her. 'You know exactly what you're doing to me. Don't make me wait any longer . . .'

At last; at long, long last, she felt his fingers slide a little further down her belly, until finally they were resting on the prominent swell of her pubis. At the first touch of his fingertips, she began trembling, sliding her thighs apart, so that her sex-lips parted and a flood of pent-up dew welled up from her womanhood, trickling out to form a damp patch on the blanket beneath her.

'I can smell your sex, Venetia,' whispered Ramon as he began to stroke her inner thighs. 'It smells good. Good enough to eat.'

His fingers climbed a little higher up her thigh, towards the crease where thigh meets groin, the very margin of a woman's sex. Venetia's womanhood pouted a welcome, the plump lips parting and the inner labia running with juice.

At first, Ramon's fingers made no attempt to explore the deeper intimacies of Venetia's sex. He stroked the silky, yellow-gold curls of her pubic hair, teasing and winding them, pulling them gently but firmly enough to provoke the most astonishing sensations.

Then she felt a fingertip slide, with an aggressive suddenness, into the tight wet haven of her sex. Its muscular walls contracted at this sudden yet welcome invasion, capturing it, refusing to let it go. But Ramon did not want to go. He wanted to possess her more completely. First one finger, then two, then three entered her vagina, stretching it so tightly that she half-thought he would tear her apart, fanning out his fingers so that they tested the elasticity of the hot, wet membranes to the very utmost.

'Oh! No don't. Please don't. I can't take it, I truly can't.'

Ramon's fingers began moving slowly inside her, twisting and turning, pressing now against the neck of her womb, now against the ring of ultra-sensitive flesh at the very entrance to her womanhood.

And then he bent over her, pressing his face between her thighs, pushing his tongue between the parted lips of her sex, seeking out the white-hot heart, the epicentre of her need.

'Ah, ah, aah!' She was squealing and shrieking with excitement now, her cries echoing across the camp-site, but she didn't care. All she cared about was Ramon's tongue-tip, winding round and round the base of her clitoris, teasing the fleshy inner folds of her sex so that the hood slid back and forth, alternately baring and concealing the head of her swollen clitoris.

'Come for me, my darling.'

'I can't. It's too much. I can't.'

'Come for me now, my love. Can't you feel it? Feel the pleasure inside you, Venetia. My fingers are right inside you, and my tongue is on your clit. All you have to do is relax, and let it happen. Let me make it good for you . . .'

His fingers and his tongue possessed her, aroused her, controlling the rhythm of her desire . . . and suddenly he was making her come, dragging the ecstasy out of her with such delicious skill that it was almost painful.

Coming, coming, coming. She could feel it bundling up inside her, that breathless excitement, that moment of suspense when the whole world stops on its axis and the only thing that exists is the desperate need to reach out and seize the pleasure.

'Yes! Oh yes!'

The orgasm tore through her like a desert wind, shaking her body like a leaf, every muscle in her body tensing, every nerve-ending screaming for the sheer, naked joy of release.

It took a long, long time for the last waves of pleasure to subside. Longer still for Venetia to come down from the incredible high which lingered on, leaving her warm and lazy and almost drugged with the aftermath of ecstasy.

They might have lain there for hours, just gently caressing each other's bodies, if the night had not suddenly been disturbed by a loud voice, coming from somewhere outside the tent.

'Miss Fellowes? Miss Venetia Fellowes?'

Venetia groaned, reaching out to pick up her silk robe – the one luxury she had allowed herself on this trip – from where it had fallen in a crumpled heap on the floor.

'Oh no,' she muttered. 'We must have woken up the neighbours. I bet old Cosgrove has complained about the noise . . .'

Ramon got up and put on his jeans while Venetia walked towards the tent-flap.

'Miss Fellowes! Police.'

'All right, all right, I'm coming.'

Venetia unzipped the tent-flap and folded it back. Two young Turkish policemen were standing outside, and their embarrassment was obvious as their eyes travelled all over the blonde Englishwoman, the curves of her body clearly visible beneath the sheer silk robe.

'Yes? What is it? If it's about the noise . . .'

The taller of the two policemen raised his hand, shaking his head.

'No, no, it is not that.' Venetia was glad he spoke good English, as she was still pretty much limited to ancient Arabic dialects. 'You will permit us to enter?'

Venetia sighed.

'Help yourself.'

She turned and led them inside the tent.

'What is the matter?' demanded Ramon, wriggling his feet into his shoes. He looked uneasy – as well he might. One or two small artefacts had been 'disappearing' from the site, and Ramon Jerez knew more about it than he might want the police to know.

Venetia shrugged.

'No idea. Something and nothing, I expect. It usually is. Maybe the Land Rover's been stolen again.'

'I am afraid we have some worrying news for you, Miss Fellowes,' began the policeman. 'We have been asked to contact you by the French police.'

The hairs on the back of Venetia's neck stood on end.

'The *French* police? What is this all about?'

'It is about your sister.'

'Cassie!' The blood drained from Venetia's face. 'Why? What's happened? Has there been some sort of accident?' She thought back to all those disturbing dreams she'd been having. She'd just *known* something bad was going to happen.

'I'm afraid we don't know. In fact, we don't know what has happened to your sister, Miss Fellowes. According to the message we have received from the French police, it would appear that she has . . . disappeared.'

Venetia sank down on to the rickety chair beside the folding table.

'Disappeared? But . . . surely you must know something.'

'Very little, madam. The friends she was staying with in Valazur reported her disappearance a few weeks ago, and nothing has been heard from her since.'

'Perhaps she's moved out,' said Venetia, searching for a rational explanation. 'Yes, that'll be it. Cassie never stays in one place for long.'

'It seems unlikely that her departure was planned, madam. You see, all her clothes and possessions were left behind. She has simply vanished without trace.'

'No!' Venetia felt Ramon's arm about her shoulders, but she did not respond to it. 'That can't be true.'

'I am sure the French police will do all they can to find her. And of course, if anything new is discovered . . .'

Venetia gently prised Ramon's arm from her shoulders and got to her feet.

'No,' she said, quietly and firmly. 'That really isn't good enough. There has to be something I can do.'

'But what?' demanded Ramon, in slight exasperation. He had heard Venetia's stories of her twin sister's exploits. This was bound to be just another of Cassie's irresponsible jaunts, going off somewhere on impulse without bothering to tell anyone. 'You have told me about your sister, Venetia. She is quite safe, I am sure. You should not worry . . .'

Venetia's eyes met Ramon's.

'This time there really is something wrong,' she said. 'I can feel it. I've known it for days . . . you know what twins are like. Sometimes there's a kind of telepathy between us. Something's happened to Cassie, and I'm going to find out what.'

'But how?'

'How do you think? I'm going to Valazur.'

Chapter Two

THE VILLAGE OF Valazur lay shimmering in the noonday sunshine as Venetia got out of the car and thanked the driver for his kindness.

She wouldn't normally have considered hitching, but after all this was an emergency, and without the luxury of a hire-car to get her around, it had proved frustratingly difficult to get to this secluded village, a few miles inland from the resorts of the French Riviera.

Venetia hadn't been quite sure what to expect, and Valazur came as quite a surprise, nestling in a valley between wooded hills, its red clay roofs roasting and sizzling in the early summer sun. At *sieste* time, the village was hardly buzzing with activity – unless you counted the sound of crickets singing among the olive trees, parasol pines and mimosa. And in any event, there wasn't a great deal *to* Valazur – just a straggling village street with a *boulangerie*, bar and *épicerie*. Narrow sidestreets lined with picturesque stone cottages led off in one direction to hillsides and open fields, in the other to the sloping road which led eventually to the coast and a narrow, pebbly beach.

Considering it was so close to the bustling Riviera resorts of Nice, Antibes and Juan-les-pins, Valazur was a remarkably sleepy, almost forgotten place, particularly at midday. Venetia could see why. The ground positively sizzled underneath her feet, and the sun was baking down on the back of her neck. This wasn't a place to work – it was a place to laze about half-naked and have fun. No wonder Cassie had written to say she liked it so much.

Cassie. The thought returned Venetia's mind briskly to the task in hand. She mustn't start thinking she'd come here on holiday – although her acid-tongued project director, Dr Cosgrove, obviously thought she had. No, she'd come here to find out exactly what had happened to her twin sister.

She walked slowly down the main street, glancing in the shop windows. She was hungry and thirsty, but at noon the shops were closed, their blinds down, and most of the cottages had their shutters firmly closed. Nothing would reopen until two or two-thirty, and she couldn't possibly last out that long. Besides, she needed to find somewhere to stay the night.

The open door of the local brasserie beckoned her in, the sounds of music and lively chatter floating out. She could smell *pastis* and garlicky *merguez* sausages. Mmm, yes. Lunch!

As she stepped through the door into the cool interior, everything seemed to freeze. Eyes turned on her, widening, mouths dropping open, a single wine-glass falling with a sharp crash as the silvery fragments flew all over the bar-room floor.

'Pour l'amour du bon Dieu . . .!'

The exclamation came from behind the bar, where a thin, grey-haired man was in the middle of pouring a glass of anisette. His face registered astonishment, tinged with alarm.

It took several seconds for Venetia to realise why everyone looked so completely stunned. Then the penny dropped. She walked up to the bar, drew out a fifty-franc note and slid it across the counter.

'Vin rouge, s'il vous plaît. Et une baguette jambon-fromage.' Her eyes travelled round the watching customers. She smiled. *'Bonjour. Je m'appelle Mademoiselle Fellowes. Mademoiselle Venetia Fellowes.'*

A palpable sigh of relief ran around the bar as the tension evaporated, and conversations started up again as though nothing at all had happened.

The barman set a glass of wine on the bar and

took a ham and cheese baguette from underneath a glass dome. Counting the change into her hand, he glanced at her quizzically.

'So, Mademoiselle, you would perhaps be the sister of *pauvre* Mademoiselle Cassandra?'

Venetia sipped her wine.

'That's right. I've come to find out what's happened to her. Do you know anything?'

She looked directly at the barman but he avoided her gaze.

'*Non*. No-one here knows anything. It is most unfortunate, yes? We cannot imagine where she has gone. We have informed the police, *bien sûr*, but . . .'

'Yes.' Venetia wondered why everyone was obviously listening to what she was saying, but avoiding looking at her. She'd always been sensitive to atmospheres, and this one felt particularly weird. Not unfriendly exactly, just weird. Like . . . just *maybe* . . . a conspiracy of silence.

She decided it would be wise to take a different tack.

'I'm looking for somewhere to stay in Valazur. Is there anywhere around here . . . not too expensive?'

The barman shrugged.

'We have rooms here. Not *grand luxe*, you understand, but *assez confortable*.'

'I could stay here, say, for a few nights?'

The barman went on polishing glasses.

'*Comme vous voulez.*'

Her resolve temporarily dented by the barman's rather uncommunicative attitude, Venetia decided to take her lunch and eat it at one of the tables she could see in the far corner of the bar. As she walked across the room she was aware of many covert glances, of eyes following her, their gazes almost like secret caresses. Never before had she been in such a strangely sexual atmosphere, a place which quite simply oozed desire.

The atmosphere was accentuated when she felt a hand slide surreptitiously across her backside, helping itself to a thorough grope of her bum before sliding away. She turned round sharply, but of course everyone was looking in the opposite direction, taking not the slightest interest in her . . . or so it seemed.

Unaccustomed to provoking such a sensation, Venetia headed to the darkest corner of the bar and sat down at a table, wriggling out of her backpack and pushing it behind her chair.

She surveyed the other customers. They were men mostly, apart from that rather chic thirtysomething brunette. She was wearing tight white shorts and a cropped top which emphasised the firmness of her small, pert breasts. Venetia felt quite blowsy by comparison. The woman's companion was a middle-aged man, quite distinguished, with dark-brown hair just beginning to grey at the temples. He was running his hand up and down the woman's thigh, slowly and very sensually . . .

But it was Venetia he was looking at.

Strangely fascinated by this little tableau, Venetia hardly noticed the figure slipping into the seat beside her until she felt his hand on her shoulder and heard his voice in her ear. A voice which was unmistakably English.

'Miss Fellowes? Venetia?'

'What?'

She swung round and was confronted by a young man of perhaps twenty-five or six, with tousled brown hair and a friendly, open face. He was wearing denims and a check shirt, the neck unbuttoned and the sleeves rolled up to the elbows.

'I'm sorry – did I startle you?'

'Well—'

'Look, I know it must seem a bit odd, coming all the way to the south of France and then being accosted in a bar by this crazy English guy. But as soon as I realised who you were, I just had to talk to you.'

'What about?'

'About . . . look, it's kind of difficult to tell you right here. It's not really safe.'

Venetia looked at him with a mixture of curiosity and suspicion. She was beginning to wonder just what was going on in Valazur.

'What do you mean, not safe?'

'There are things . . . things you ought to know about. Frankly, it would have been a lot better if you hadn't come here in the first place, but now you're here . . .'

'Are you trying to warn me off?' demanded Venetia.

'No! Or at least, not in the way you think I am. I'm just worried about your safety.'

'I'm a grown-up woman, thanks very much. I can take care of myself.'

'Yeah.' The young man stared into his glass. 'I bet that's what Cassie said, too.'

'What do you know about Cassie? Do you know what's happened to her?'

'I . . . no, I don't. But let's just say I've got my suspicions. I can tell you what I know . . . but I can't tell you here. I'm renting rooms in Cap Carlotte, it's just a couple of miles down the coast from here. If you could come with me . . .'

Venetia shook her head. 'Just hang on, Mr Whatever-your-name-is. I'm not going anywhere with a complete stranger. And certainly not unless you can tell me more. How do I know it's not you who's responsible for Cassie's disappearance?'

The stranger sighed. 'Look. I understand what you're saying, but like I said, it's dangerous to talk here. My name's Evan Peterson, and I'm a freelance jounalist. That's all I dare tell you.' He leaned forward across the table. 'Get out of this place, Venetia. Don't stay. If you do, you'll regret it.'

Venetia got to her feet. She didn't like the way this conversation was heading. 'Are you threatening me, Mr Peterson?'

Peterson let out a gasp of exasperation. 'Don't talk crap, of course I'm not! I'm just trying to protect you, that's all.'

'I can manage, thanks.' Venetia turned to leave. 'If you've got something important to say, why don't you tell it to the police?'

Peterson sat back in his chair, running his fingers through his hair. 'Go and talk to them yourself, Venetia. Go and have a little chat with Inspector Defarge. Maybe then you'll understand why.'

That evening, after a long and frustrating afternoon, Venetia came back to the bar. She was beginning to wish she hadn't been so curt with Peterson. Now she could understand why he'd been so dismissive about the local constabulary.

Oh, they'd been friendly enough on the surface – positively helpful even. Yes, her sister had disappeared. Yes, they were doing all they could to find her. No, they hadn't any leads. None at all, but they were doing their best, and of course, if there was any news . . .

But there was something obstructive about Inspector Defarge. Something he wasn't telling her, almost as if he suspected that something bad had happened to Cassie but wasn't saying. The last straw had been when he'd made a clumsy pass at her, telling her how attractive she was, and then trying to stroke her breasts! Even if you accepted all the old clichés about libidinous Frenchmen, the little Riviera village of Valazur seemed to have an unusually lively interest in sex.

As she drank alone in Gérard's Bar, she wondered what she was going to do next. What could she do that the police hadn't already done? Or had they really done anything at all? Maybe she should have done what Peterson asked and gone to his apartment? Well, no doubt she'd see him again.

Gérard, the bar-owner, conducted his typically terse conversation as he cut a lemon into wafer-thin slices with a Sabatier table-knife.

'You have had no success today, Mademoiselle Fellowes?'

'No luck, Gérard.'

'You go home to England now?'

'Not yet,' replied Venetia, half-amused and half-exasperated. Why was everyone so keen to get rid of her? 'I'm not giving up yet – I've only been here one day!'

The barman's expression changed as a customer came into the bar.

'Ah, Monsieur Bastien!' he smarmed, as eager to please as a small lapdog. '*Quel plaisir de vous accueillir.*'

The newcomer was a tall, impossibly elegant man in his mid-thirties; wavy, golden-brown hair streaked blond by the sun framing a tanned face with strong features and grey-blue eyes. He was sophisticated even in casual clothes, the cut of his light summer shirt and trousers emphasising the sinuous lines of his athletic body.

As he sauntered up to the bar, he flashed Venetia an appreciative smile.

'*Bonsoir, Mademoiselle.*'

She nodded her acknowledgement as he bought a *bière blonde* and poured it into the glass, turning towards her and leaning casually on the bar-top.

'Monsieur.' In the recesses of her mind she was searching for a memory. Bastien? Where had she heard that name before?

'This is Mademoiselle Venetia Fellowes, Monsieur Bastien.' The barman nudged the newcomer's arm and nodded in Venetia's direction. 'The sister of Mademoiselle Cassandra . . .'

'Indeed.' Bastien put down his drink, reached out and took Venetia's hand, pressing it to his lips. 'The resemblance is most striking. *Enchanté*, Mademoiselle Fellowes. Allow me to introduce myself to you properly. My name is Bastien Le Rocq. Cassie and I were friends before she . . .' He hesitated. 'As you perhaps know, your sister was a guest at my villa at the time of her disappearance.'

Realisation dawned. Of course! How could she have been so dim-witted? Cassie had mentioned that some wealthy acquaintance had invited her to spend a few days at his villa. So this was the delicious Bastien. Venetia could see how a girl might lose her head over him . . .

'You were there when she vanished?'

'*Hélas, non.* I returned from a business trip to find the whole village in an uproar. It seems she just walked out into the night, and never returned. It was a great shock to us all. I really am most sorry. I feel . . . *dans une certaine mesure* . . . responsible for what has happened.' He paused, gazing thoughtfully into the bottom of his glass then taking a long drink. 'Whatever has happened. I wish I knew where she has gone, and if she will return.'

'So do I,' sighed Venetia. Her heart had leapt at the realisation that this was Cassie's friend . . . and most probably her lover, too. Cassie preferred her friendships to be intimate. But whatever the nature of their relationship had been, it was obvious that Bastien, charming though he might be, knew nothing about Cassie's disappearance.

'Mademoiselle . . .?'

'Please, call me Venetia. I feel as if I know you

already – through my sister.'

'Indeed. I was wondering, Venetia . . . You are staying here in the village tonight?'

'Yes.'

'I was wondering if you might do me the honour of dining with me this evening. At the Villa Le Rocq.'

An anticipatory shiver ran over Venetia's body; a shiver which had nothing at all to do with the cooling breeze filtering in through the open door of the bar. Bastien Le Rocq was undeniably gorgeous: a hint of muscle rippling beneath flesh tanned a deep and lustrous gold by the Mediterranean sunshine; a sexy voice husky with the lilt of a French accent softened by an English education; sensual lips which simply begged to be kissed. And she could see from the glint in his eyes that his interest in her was no more platonic than hers in him. If she went to his villa for dinner, who could say what else might happen between them?

But hold on . . . This man was Cassie's friend – no, Cassie's lover. It wouldn't be right. She wouldn't go, she mustn't.

'Well . . .,' she smiled, a frisson of excitement thrilling through her body. And then she heard herself say: 'Thank you, Bastien. I'd be delighted.'

Bastien Le Rocq's villa stood on the very edge of Valazur, set among groves of olive and lemon trees in the lee of the surrounding wooded hills.

Venetia had never seen anything like the Villa Le Rocq – at least, not outside the covers of *Hello!* magazine. It was a vast, white-painted, modern building with so many wings and extensions that it looked more like an exclusive hotel or administrative complex than one man's home.

They roared up the long driveway in Bastien's pre-war Hispano-Suiza, a magnificent thing of chrome and brass and bright red paint, which purred like a sleeping tiger as they slid smoothly over the bumpy ground.

'I just use it as a runabout,' he explained, as they swung around and parked in front of the villa. 'I have other cars, of course, but this adds a touch of romance to one's life, don't you think?'

'I . . . yes.' Venetia felt tongue-tied, and just a little giggly – certainly in no fit state to ask Bastien any coherent questions about Cassie. It didn't help that he had plied her with champagne back at the bar, and Venetia *adored* champagne – particularly vintage Veuve Clicquot, which Bastien seemed to regard as a necessity of life, rather than a luxury.

So she felt rather pleasantly light-headed as Bastien opened the car door for her and she stepped out. Not drunk, just tipsy enough to have forgotten all her inhibitions – and Ramon.

A black-suited butler was waiting to take their coats and usher them into a rather exquisite sitting-room, the restrained pastel decor setting off the authentic art deco furniture and collectibles. There was no dining-table, but a small side-table had been set with a white cloth and sparkling silver cutlery.

'Please, Venetia, be perfectly at your ease. Would you care for a drink before Joseph serves us with dinner?'

'Well ... I don't think I should really. Not after ...'

'Nonsense. *Un tout petit peu de champagne ...*' Bastien reached for a bottle, already put on ice – no doubt by the conveniently telepathic Joseph – and began unscrewing the wire cage.

'Oh, Bastien, I really shouldn't. More champagne! I think I've had quite enough already, don't you?'

He looked into her eyes, and she felt suddenly lost, adrift on an ocean of desire.

'One can never have enough champagne, *ma chère* Venetia. Or enough nights of love with a beautiful woman.'

His words seemed to slice into her heart like blades of surgical steel, ruthlessly searching out her desire and laying it bare. Could she keep no secrets from this man? She could feel what little resistance she had had, weakening by the second. She tried to gather up what remained of her composure, keeping her voice calm and even.

'Is that your philosophy of life, Bastien?'

He laughed, but there was a depth of

seriousness beyond the merriment, his blue-grey eyes velvety and soft and so very, very compelling.

'Of life, of love . . . *enfin*, of everything. I believe in living life to the full, and enjoying only the best. This champagne, for example, is the finest vintage that money can buy. And you, my dear Venetia, are a sublimely beautiful woman.'

This time, as she returned his gaze, she felt desire burst forth from her like water escaping from a dam, breaking down her resistance, forcing her to acknowledge, in the silence of her thoughts, that her body was responding powerfully and joyously to Bastien Le Rocq.

The cork exploded from the champagne-bottle in a shower of white fizz, and Bastien deftly caught the first of the wine in a glass, filling it to the brim and handing it to Venetia.

She made no further protest. Bastien was right – the iced champagne was wonderful, and what's more he was tremendously good company. It was no use ignoring the excitement in her belly, the itch of need between her thighs, and she found herself surreptitiously pressing together her thighs, intensifying the pleasure of her arousal.

Bastien sipped his champagne, looking at Venetia pensively.

'How curious. You are exactly like your sister . . . and yet so completely different.'

Venetia smiled.

'Cassie's the outrageous one. I'm just ordinary. Pretty unadventurous really.'

'Really?' Bastien raised a sceptical eyebrow. 'It is true, perhaps, that on the surface you are quieter . . . subtler than your sister. More mature too. But I can sense a great passion within you. You are a deeply sensual woman, Venetia Fellowes.'

She stared at him, shocked and excited by his words. No man had ever spoken to her like this before – and she had only just met Bastien Le Rocq! They were almost perfect strangers – and she wasn't even sure that she liked him. Yet what she had said to him was true – she did feel as though she knew him, if only through the friendship he had had with Cassie.

'You are very kind,' she said, her voice trembling a little as Bastien laid his hand upon hers.

'I am never kind, *ma chère*. To be kind is to be dishonest. I am merely stating what I see.' He glanced out into the gardens, a soft, dusky green in the gathering twilight. 'Would you care to walk with me in the garden before dinner?'

Without waiting for her reply, he pressed a concealed switch and the glass doors slid open on silent runners, letting in the deliciously balmy evening air. He reached out and took her by the hand, leading her outside as though she were a timorous child. She hadn't felt this awkward in the company of a man since she was a teenage virgin – a gauche kid very nearly seduced by her riding instructor on her fifteenth birthday. In the end it had been Cassie who had given her virginity to him – but then Cassie had never regarded virginity as anything other than an impediment to pleasure.

There was something about Bastien Le Rocq which made Venetia recall her sister's first lover. Maybe it was that same quality which had attracted Cassie to Bastien . . . and which was now making Venetia so very hot for him.

Or maybe she was reading too much into the situation. Maybe Bastien was just flattering her because he felt bad about Cassie's disappearance. Or maybe he really did want her. And as she looked into his eyes, Venetia saw how eloquently they spoke of his desire. The excitement of that look, that touch, that fleeting caress as his hand brushed lightly over the side of her breast, made her head swim with something far more intoxicating than an alcoholic haze. She tried to think of ways of beginning an ordinary conversation with this man she wanted so much to kiss her.

'You have a beautiful home, Bastien.'

His smile turned her legs to jelly, and made her nipples tingle under the tight fabric of her simple black Lycra minidress. She wished she had brought something more sophisticated with her, but then she hadn't bargained on being invited to dinner by Bastien Le Rocq.

'You are most kind.' Bastien and Venetia stood looking out over the gardens, the scents of flowers and fruits and herbs surrounding them in a caressing warmth. 'I have been rather fortunate in my business dealings, that is all.' He laughed good-humouredly. 'What is it you say in English? The luck of the Devil?'

'I'm sure you must have worked very hard,' protested Venetia.

Bastien thrust his hands into his pockets and they strolled together among the softly rustling trees.

'*Ma chère*, I never give less than one hundred per cent.' His eyes met Venetia's. 'In anything.'

The grounds of the Villa Le Rocq were laid out in an informal style, using the natural slopes and curves of the terrain to form miniature hills and valleys. Tree-lined groves and copses, riots of brilliantly-coloured flowers, climbing roses and great hanging drifts of bougainvillea and passi-flora . . . this was a man-made paradise kept eternally fresh and beautiful by a small, silent army of gardeners.

'Let me show you my favourite part of the garden, Venetia.'

They passed together through an archway, almost hidden by tangles of leaves and flowers, and entered a small glade. In the centre was a sunken pond, filled with silvery fish whose scales turned to iridescent rainbows as they wriggled in the water. A tiny spring and waterfall constantly refreshed the pool, filling the glade with the soft splashing of running water. Greek and Roman statues, their features softened by the ravages of time, kept watch from among the trees, their sightless eyes forever open, their bodies inter-twined in postures of love.

'Many of these statues were taken from Pompeii,' explained Bastien. 'They were housed in the Villa of Venus – a house of pleasure. You do not object to my taste in erotic art?'

'I . . .'

'No, my dear Venetia, of course you do not. For you share your sister's love of all things sensual and beautiful.' He took Venetia's hand and drew her to him. She wondered if he could feel the raw, naked desire throbbing out from the heart of her. 'Sit down beside me, Venetia.'

They sat together on an ornately carved stone bench, very old, weathered by time and covered in places by soft cushions of fresh green moss and greyish-orange scales of lichen. Her hand was still in his, and she wondered why she felt no wish to draw away. This was not like her. She had come here to ask questions about Cassie, not to let herself be seduced by the first man who showed an interest in her.

But then Bastien Le Rocq wasn't just any man,

was he? He was aesthetically beautiful, an irresistible erotic temptation for any woman, especially a woman like Venetia Fellows. But she couldn't. No; really she couldn't . . .

'I am very sorry about Cassie, Venetia. I will do all I can to help you find her.'

Quite unexpectedly, he took Venetia's face between his hands and kissed her, very tenderly, on the lips. Venetia started shaking at his touch, involuntarily drawing back from the kiss even though she wanted it more than anything.

'You are afraid of me?'

She shook her head although, in all honesty, she was perhaps just a little afraid of Bastien Le Rocq.

'Not afraid. Guilty.'

'*Mais . . . pourquoi?*'

'My sister. You and she were . . .' She searched Bastien's face for the answer she wanted. 'Weren't you?'

Bastien raised his hands then let them fall to his thighs.

'It is true that we once made love,' he replied. 'One night, one night only. But it was a mistake, Venetia. Cassie and I were meant only to be friends, we talked about it, she told me she understood. We were never lovers, Venetia. Never lovers in a way that you and I might be.'

He touched her again. Her whole body seemed to vibrate at the touch of his fingers, the lightest

47

caress sending shockwaves of excitement right through her, to her very core. Her head was spinning, the champagne lulling her, soothing her, seducing her even before Bastien had kissed her again.

'Bastien . . . no please, you mustn't.'

'But Venetia, *ma petite*, you know how much you want me. As much as I want you. The first moment I saw you I knew we were destined to share a glorious passion.'

'Bastien . . . oh . . .'

He took her in his arms and crushed his mouth against hers, the point of his long, muscular tongue forcing its way between her lips like a miniature penis. She had never had such kisses before. Oh, she had lovers enough, some of them – like Ramon – skilful and passionate. But none of them kissed like Bastien Le Rocq.

Their tongues met and slid over each other, the wetness of their saliva mingling, tangy and sharp from the champagne. Bastien's hunger for her was astonishing, terrifying and wonderful all at once, and she responded instinctively, her tongue exploring his mouth, her lips wet from their shared passion.

The kiss seemed to last a long, long time, and then their lips parted, reluctantly and slowly. A tiny smudge of Venetia's red lipstick had found its way on to Bastien's cheek and she put out her tongue and began licking it off, adoring the slight sensation of roughness. She was panting a little, her breath halting and rapid.

Bastien caught hold of her fingers and put them to his lips, at first just kissing the tips very lightly, then opening his mouth and sliding them inside, sucking on them, licking and biting them. She writhed with unexpected delight, discovering the world of sensation in her fingers, the incredible tingle of excitement as his tongue ran over their very tips.

At last he released her fingers and began darting light kisses on the underside of her hand, from fingers to palm to wrist, and then down the long, creamy sweep of Venetia's bare arm.

She could not speak; Bastien had robbed her of any words to describe the pleasure she was feeling. With just a kiss on her fingertips he had completed her seduction. Now, she knew in her heart, she would do anything, abolutely anything, for a chance to feel Bastien Le Rocq's manhood sliding into the warm, welcoming depths of her sex.

He reached her shoulder and kissed it lightly, sliding down the shoulder-strap of her dress so that it hung down over her upper arm, and the neckline hung a little lower on that side, revealing more of the white globe of her breast.

'There is such a charming innocence to you, *ma chère*,' whispered Bastien. 'Cassie is a flirt, a woman who likes to control men. But you,

Venetia, you are like a sensual child in a woman's body, greedy for love and yet so, so virginal.'

Venetia thrilled to his touch as he slipped down the other strap of her dress and began kissing and licking her right shoulder.

'Bastien . . . oh Bastien . . .' she groaned as lust raged in her belly, caressing Bastien's smooth golden-brown hair. And Bastien silently took her right hand and slid it down until it was between his thighs.

'Feel what you do to me, *chérie*. It is all for you. And it wants so much to be inside you.'

She ran her fingers over the long, hard swelling beneath the crisp linen of Bastien's pants. It was so thick – too thick to encircle with the fingers of one hand. A battering-ram of flesh that would stretch any womanhood, no matter how wet or how willing.

'Your cock is beautiful,' heard herself murmuring. Dizzy with drink and desire, it was like hearing some other woman speaking her words.

'Not as beautiful as your breasts,' replied Bastien. 'They are so full and so firm. Would you allow me to look at them?'

'Yes, oh yes. Please . . .'

He peeled down the front of her dress with infinite slowness, not once touching the flesh beneath. There could be no thoughts of modesty or coyness, not any more. She was wearing no bra, and excitement had turned her nipples to iron-hard nubs which yearned to be kissed. But no kisses came. Bastien just looked at them, running his eyes over them again and again. The waiting was unbearable.

'May I touch your breasts, Venetia?'

This time he did not wait for her to reply, and cupped her breasts in his hands, weighing them as though they were heavy fruits, testing their firmness and their ripe succulence.

'You have the most astonishingly beautiful breasts, Venetia. Such pure, white flesh; and they are so firm, so adorably kissable. I so want to kiss your breasts.'

'Take them in your mouth. Kiss my nipples, please, hurry, I can't bear it!'

As Bastien's lips closed about her right nipple, Venetia felt a rush of juice gushing from her sex and moistening the white cotton triangle of her panties. She shuffled her backside on the stone bench, feeling its coldness seeping up into her, but never quite deep enough to soothe the burning of her sex or the aching need of her secret gateway, the amber rose concealed in the shadowy valley between her buttocks.

Bastien's hand slid to her thigh, and started ruching up the hem of her dress. It clung so tightly to her stocking-clad thighs that it seemed to take an age before he revealed the bare flesh between lacy black stocking-tops and panties.

Venetia felt utterly shameless. Every inhibition

she had ever had seemed to have disappeared, evaporating in a haze of champagne and lascivious desire. Her fingers crept up over the crotch of Bastien's pants, until she found the tag of his zipper and, taking it between finger and thumb, she eased it down over his penis.

An appreciative shiver tensed Bastien's body at the moment when her fingers slipped through the front opening of his silk shorts and released the thick, stiff rod from its imprisonment. It felt hot and smooth in her hand, like living stone, hard and unforgiving. How she longed to have it inside her, to satisfy the gnawing hunger which made her hips grind and her back arch at Bastien's touch.

Letting her nipple escape from between his teeth, Bastien moved on, his tongue describing a widening spiral around the fleshy dome, then diving deep into the valley between her breasts, leaving a gloss of saliva which felt oddly cool in the warm night air.

'You have the devil in your fingers,' groaned Bastien as Venetia slowly masturbated him, her caresses making him even harder and thicker, the girth of his prick swelling with each long, luxurious stroke.

A clear, glossy juice was trickling over the ripe plum of Bastien's glans. Venetia smoothed her fingers over it, making him growl with appreciative lust, using the slick wetness to lubricate the whole of his straining, curving shaft.

'I have to have you, *ma chère* . . .'

'I want you too.'

'Will you let me come inside you?'

'Oh yes, I want you, I can't wait much longer.'

She sank back on to the bench. Bastien was on top of her, his hands sliding and rolling the skirt of her minidress high on to her hips. She couldn't believe how much she wanted him. It wasn't simple desire any more, it was a savage hunger – it felt as if she had to have this man, right here and now, or she would die of frustrated need.

Bastien's fingers traced the line of her suspender, leading from the top of her black stocking, across the bare, creamy flesh of her upper thigh, to the crease of her groin. Her plump labia, engorged with need, pushed hard against the tight cotton of her white panties. She could feel that the gusset was wringing wet with her juices, and knew that the thin material must be well-nigh transparent, revealing every intimate secret of her womanhood.

Not that this was any time to think of secrets. Bastien's fingertips were stroking along her groin, following the line of her panties, diving down to caress her through the wet gusset.

'Such a pretty sight, Venetia,' whispered Bastien. His voice sounded faraway, as though they were both in some wildly erotic dream, where her every thought and wish came true. 'It is so beautiful to see a woman's sex through her wet panties, to smell her desire, to rub her through the wet material and make her still wetter.'

His fingers brushed very lightly over the wet fabric, never pressing hard enough to bring her to orgasm, but tormenting her with caresses which aroused and excited beyond belief.

'Touch me. Touch me there,' pleaded Venetia, making him press his hand harder against her pubis.

'Like this, *chérie*?' He began rubbing with a smooth, circular motion, pressing harder and harder on the hypersensitive flesh around her clitoris, making her sweat and squeal with uncontrollable desire.

'Oh yes, yes, yes!' Her hips lifted a fraction off the stone bench, straining to push against Bastien's fingers, making him masturbate her harder, faster, bringing her closer and closer to the point of no return.

'I want to fuck you,' he whispered, lowering himself over her, so that his face was very close to hers. He planted kisses on her bare throat. 'I want to fuck you right now, Venetia Fellowes.'

Slipping his finger under the edge of her panties, he encountered the hot wet lake of her womanhood.

'I think you want it too,' he smiled.

How could she deny it? Her poor clitoris was

throbbing and burning, her vulva so full of its own juices that her panties and now the hem of her dress were sodden. Oh yes, she wanted it. She wanted it so much she could hardly breathe for the need of his cock inside her.

'Come inside me,' she murmured.

His fingers pushed aside the gusset of her panties, now scarcely more than an irrelevant scrap of wet cotton. No need to take them off, all he needed to do was ease them across the swollen lips of her vulva, baring the full beauty of her sex. Her golden-blonde curls were darker with wetness, and had formed themselves into glossy clumps and tendrils which clung to the sex-swollen flesh.

Her inner labia were a deep pink, between coral and magenta, swollen with the blood which had turned her small, discreet clitoris into a hard, menacing spike. Sexual release; she needed it, she wanted it, she must have it. Now.

The tip of Bastien's penis probed the soft wet interior of her sex, nudging gently between its welcoming lips, pushing lightly, not too fast, gently now . . .

'Aah! Oh Bastien, I can't . . .'

She tried to wriggle away, but Bastien was relentless. She hadn't thought the thickness of his shaft would feel so huge, stretching her almost to the point of fear as he slid smoothly into her.

'*Courage, ma petite, ça y est.*' Bastien kissed her as

the last inch of his stiff prick slid inside her, tighter than a hand in a leather glove.

Now that he was inside her, if felt so good that Venetia wondered why she had been afraid. As he moved within her, the rhythm of his cock in and out of her stimulated the nerve-endings around the entrance to her vagina, filling her with an incredible tumult of sensations. And the hairy sac of his balls pressed against her vulva with each new stroke, tickling and teasing her into the sweetest pleasure.

She was drifting now, drifting on a warm, sweet tide. Why fight it? Cassie and Bastien had been friends, that was all. And now Venetia and Bastien were lovers . . . for one night, at least. She wasn't naive enough to think that he was her dream man – a man like Bastien Le Rocq was not for her – but for tonight at least this incredible pleasure was her dream made real, and she didn't care if she never woke up.

Chapter Three

THE NEXT MORNING, Venetia awoke in Bastien Le Rocq's bed.

She opened her eyes to find him standing beside her, impeccably handsome as ever in a towelling robe, and carrying a tray with two glasses and a bottle of wine.

'More wine! Bastien, you mustn't. I had far too much champagne last night. I can hardly remember . . .'

His face assumed an expression of disappointment, but his eyes were twinkling as he set down the tray, turned back the white satin sheets and slid into bed beside her.

'You don't remember, *chérie*? You don't remember how we made passionate love in the garden, and poor Joseph had to throw our dinner away? And then later, when we came upstairs and . . . you really don't remember?'

'I remember that you got me half-drunk on champagne and then seduced me,' replied Venetia. The disapproving pout she attempted turned into a coquettish smile. This was dreadful! She was behaving exactly like Cassie. 'And I remember enough to know that I enjoyed it. But really, I'd better leave now. I have so much to do, and Gérard will be wondering why my bed's not been slept in.'

'I doubt it,' replied Bastien with a knowing smile. 'And in any case, Gérard can go to hell. Why don't you move in here for a few days, *chérie*, as my guest? It's much more comfortable than that terrible poky room above the bar.'

'Oh Bastien, I couldn't.'

'Of course you could! And you must. I have already asked Joseph to prepare a guest-room. It is the least I can do after what has happened to your sister. Besides, this afternoon I must leave on a business trip to Italy. I shall not be returning until Friday . . .' His eyes sparkled. 'So you need have no fear. Your spotless English reputation will not be in danger, *Mademoiselle* Venetia.'

'You're teasing me, you beast!' Venetia picked up a pillow and moved to hit Bastien with it, but he caught it in mid-air and wrestled Venetia down onto the bed, pinning her arms with his strong hands.

'Do you submit, *ma chère*?'

'Never!'

'Then you must take the consequences.'

Bastien bent down and started licking her breasts. Venetia had thought last night's adventurous love-making had exhausted them both, but her breasts were unbelievably sensitive to his kisses, and as he began seducing her all over again, she saw his robe fall open, baring the swollen staff of his penis.

'Bastien . . . is this any way for a gentleman to behave?' Venetia was half-laughing, half-moaning with lust.

'Ah, *mademoiselle*, I am no gentleman. I am . . . how would you say? . . . a vile seducer.'

She grabbed hold of him and they rolled sideways on to the bed, facing each other on the rumpled sheets. Slowly and deliberately, Venetia unknotted the belt of Bastien's robe, then eased it down and back, gradually revealing his nakedness.

'Now we're quits,' she told him. And she took his nipple between her teeth and began biting it, quite hard; not hard enough to cause real pain but just enough to drive a man wild.

'*Diablesse!*' exclaimed Bastien. 'You cannot be an Englishwoman, you are a wild beast, a demon!'

Venetia smiled.

'And what sort of a man is it who has mirrors on his bedroom ceiling?'

Bastien looked deep into her eyes.

'A man who loves to watch himself making love.' His fingers stroked down Venetia's flank. 'A man who loves to watch his lover's body joining with his own, to see the sweat trickling down over her breasts, her thighs tensing and thrusting, her nipples getting so, so hard.'

Venetia let out a little sigh of pleasure as Bastien slid his fingers up the inside of her thigh and stroked her, just below the fringed margin of her labia. As she parted her thighs to let him in, his caresses released the potent scent of a long nights coupling, a heady mixture of spicy-sweet sex-juices and the salty tang of stale semen. The scene evoked fragmented memories of a long, delicious night.

'Don't you love to watch youself, Venetia?' Bastien demanded. 'Look up at yourself now, watch me caressing you.

She lay back on the bed and gazed up at the bank of mirrors covering the ceiling. Bastien had clearly spared no expense in catering for his sexual pleasure. Sixteen separate mirrors spanned the ceiling, each one tilted at a slightly different angle so that they reflected sixteen different images.

Sixteen different images of Venetia Fellowes, lying naked on a bed, while a handsome stranger slipped his fingers inside her vagina.

'Look, Venetia . . . do you see? I'm putting my finger right inside you. I'm opening you up like a beautiful flower. Spread your legs wider, my darling. I want you to see it all. Everything.'

Far from being scandalised, Venetia found herself enthralled by the images above her. It was like watching herself performing in an erotic movie, a shameless, silent performance for which there was an audience of two.

It felt so good, too. Better by far than any film. To lie there and look up and see yourself being finger-fucked, and all the time to be able to feel everything too . . . Bastien was right. There was a special pleasure in watching yourself make love.

Sliding his finger out of Venetia's sex, Bastien kissed it then held it to Venetia's lips. It was glossy with juice, fragrant as sun-ripened fruits in some Mediterranean grove.

'Kiss your desire, Venetia *ma chère*. Have you ever tasted the pleasure of a woman's sex?'

'Never.' There was almost a note of regret in Venetia's voice. Here, now, lying on this bed with the summer sunshine flooding over their naked bodies, even the thought of kissing and licking another woman's sex seemed unbelievably exciting.

'Kiss your own sex, Venetia. Taste its juices, lick them from my finger. Look – can you see in the mirror what you're doing?'

She put out her tongue, at first tentatively, and

took a little lick of juice from Bastien's finger. The taste was powerful, sweet as honey yet redolent with a hundred other flavours and perfumes – cinnamon and cloves, wild garlic and sun-warmed gorse, lavender and chocolate and blackberry and so many others that had no names, mingled with the taste of Bastien's seed.

Greedily she engulfed his finger, sucking and biting and licking it until every drop of juice had gone and her mouth was filled with the taste of fucking.

She could feel juice trickling between her labia, wetting her thighs and the satin sheet on which she was lying. Looking up at the mirrors she saw a woman in an ecstasy of torment, her face crazed with lust, every muscle in her body tensed in desperate anticipation of glorious, ultimate pleasure.

'You want me, Venetia. You do, don't you?'

'I want you.'

It was no use denying it. Her body was already responding for her, her areolae puckered and erect, her thighs spread wide, her inner labia glistening with honeydew, the secrets of her desire so shamelessly exposed.

She was puzzled when Bastien rolled away and slid down to the end of the bed, sitting himself down on the edge. He beckoned to her to join him.

'*Viens vite, ma chère*. Hurry, I am hungry for you.'

She joined him and he winked at her.

'*Assieds-toi.*'

'What?'

'Sit down . . . here, on my lap.'

He was stroking his penis, it's shaft thick and hard, the balls beneath it hanging heavy in their soft, wrinkled purse. The tip of his cock glistened with slick wetness, its clubbed head fat and purple and juicy, its single eye brimming with endless teardrops of desire.

Her heart was pounding. There was something wonderfully wicked about all of this. She had come here intending to question Bastien Le Rocq, and instead had ended up having sex with him. And now, even after she had sobered up, she was still here, going along with his ingeniously perverse games of lust. And getting more excited than she might have liked to admit.

She sat astride Bastien's lap, facing away from him, with her legs on either side of his thighs. Holding apart the plump lips of her pussy, she felt for the tip of Bastien's cock and sank down on to it in a single, blissful action which sent ripples of sheer ecstasy running through her body.

'*Ah, ma chère, ma très chère Venetia.*' Bastien's voice was a purr of satisfaction, and it excited Venetia to realise just how much power her sexuality gave her over this wealthy and exceptionally desirable man.

She was under no illusions, of course, that

Bastien Le Rocq might feel something more for her than just old-fashioned lust. After all, that was all she felt for him. No, this was glorious but it would not last. What mattered was the here and now, and the pleasure boiling and bubbling in their loins.

In front of them was a tall wardrobe in the present style, and in front of that a mahogany-framed cheval mirror. It was positioned to afford a perfect view of their coupling, and to Venetia there was something more shocking, more erotic still about this face-to-face, life-size image than there was about the mosaic of mirror-images above the bed. It was like looking through a window and seeing another self, doing all the things she had always dreamed of doing but had somehow never dared.

'That's it, my darling, lift yourself up a little further; I'll support you, I'm holding you fast.'

Bastien's hands were on her waist, helping her to raise and lower herself on his upraised penis. As she raised herself above his lap, so that only the tip of his prick was still inside her, she gazed into the mirror and saw the glistening shaft slide into view, wet with their mingled juices, smooth and veiny as pink onyx.

Then she was sliding down again, the cock-shaft disappearing, slowly swallowed up by her greedy womanhood. It felt so good, so wickedly good. She was in control and the slower she kept the pace, the better it felt. She was savouring each new sensation, making it last, turning it into a delicious eternity of waiting.

'Touch yourself,' Bastien whispered in her ear. 'I want to see you touch yourself.'

He took hold of her hand and slid it between her thighs.

'Show me, Venetia. Show me how you pleasure yourself when you have no man to pleasure you.'

Her willing fingers slipped between the outer lips of her sex, feeling with unerring precision for the hard nub of her desire. How many times had she felt for that hot, wet bud? How many times had she rubbed and stroked and caressed herself to orgasm? But never, never had she dreamed of doing this . . .

Sweat trickled down her forehead, drenching her long blonde hair; trickled down into the valley between her quivering, jiggling breasts; into the little well where the base of her spine met the top of her curving buttocks, making her skin glow and shimmer in the morning sunshine.

And the woman in the mirror smiled and laughed, tossing back her blonde locks as she masturbated, her slender fingers sliding in and out of her sex, her thighs tensing and relaxing as she rose and fell on her lover's erect penis.

Then she felt it. Bastien's hand, sliding down her back and over her buttocks, into the deep and secret valley, seeking out the hidden pleasure-garden, the amber rose which at once longed for and feared his touch.

His finger stroked along the deep furrow, skating across the secret well of sexual desire, scooping up Venetia's own juice and using it to lubricate the tight and secret sphincter.

It twitched and tensed as he touched it, and Venetia shuddered, her back arching, her breasts thrusting out.

'No, no, Bastien – not that, no, please . . . oh, oh, oh!'

His fingertip penetrated her with expert ease, though she was virgin-tight and the muscles of her anus fought to resist him. In seconds he was inside her, and suddenly she was welcoming him, delighting in this double invasion. Pleasure, pleasure, forbidden pleasure . . . it felt so good.

And the woman in the mirror cried out in ecstasy, her sex tensing in the first, delicious spasms of ecstasy.

It was late that evening, when Bastien had driven off towards Italy in a brand-new silver Mercedes, that his glamorous young cousin Léonore knocked at the door of Venetia's room and asked if she would like to visit an exclusive private casino just outside Nice.

As they drove towards the town, Léonore told Venetia a little more about Valazur.

'You mustn't mind the locals,' she grinned.

'They are ignorant peasants – Bastien is always saying so.'

'Some of them seemed quite hostile towards me,' remarked Venetia.

Léonore shrugged. 'They are foolish and superstitious. They think that when one twin has disappeared the other must follow, and that bad luck will be brought upon the village. There is said to be a great magical power in twins, you know.'

Venetia raised a quizzical eyebrow. 'Really?'

'*Mais oui* – but that is just one of the old legends. This part of France is full of them. You must take no notice of the local people – they will soon change their minds and grow to love you, as they grew to love Cassie.'

'Did you know Cassie?' Venetia as they parked the car and walked towards the entrance to the Casino.

'A little.' Léonore ran her slender fingers through her brown locks. 'But she was Bastien's friend really, not mine.'

Venetia raised a quizzical eyebrow.

'Friend?'

Léonore chuckled and patted Venetia's hand.

'Friend, *ma chère*. I do not think they were lovers – at least not for long. Cassie was not . . . *is* not Bastien's type, she is too flighty, too . . . insubstantial.'

Venetia nodded. 'Cassie always believed in

acting first and thinking later,' she sighed. 'I just hope that this time, it hasn't got her into more trouble than she can handle.'

The casino overlooked the sea, waters of deep indigo splashing gently under a moonlit sky of midnight-blue velvet. The sounds of merriment drifted across as an open-topped sports car roared past, full of beautiful, laughing, rich young people. It seemed so glamorous and carefree here. Exactly the sort of place that Cassie would love to bits. So why on earth would she suddenly up sticks and leave, without even taking her backpack with her?

Still lost in thought, Venetia followed Léonore through the ornate entrance hall, where her name was entered in the visitors' book, and left her jacket with the cloakroom attendant. As she and Léonore freshened up in the gilded powder-room, Venetia wished – not for the first time – that she had brought something to wear that was worthy of this opulent place. All she had with her, apart from the black Lycra number, was this plain blue silk shift – terribly ordinary, and not a sequin in sight. If she was intending to do any more of this sort of thing, her budget would have to stretch to a glitzier wardrobe.

Not that she was planning on staying at the Villa Le Rocq – or at least, she might stay until Bastien returned from his business trip, but then it would be time to say so long. Fun was what they had had, and she didn't want to risk it developing into anything heavier.

Still, Léonore seemed nice enough and this was certainly an opportunity to see how the other half lived. She'd never been in a casino before – though she had once helped to excavate an ancient Assyrian gaming palace.

Passing through a rather tacky room filled with noisy Americans and one-armed bandits, they reached the relative tranquillity of the main gaming saloon. They wandered between the tables, watching the gamblers placing their bets. Venetia was fascinated by their swiftly-changing expressions: the hunger, the anticipation, the elation . . . and the black despondency. It all happened so quickly, with fortunes won and lost in the space of a few minutes.

At the roulette table an immaculately dressed croupier was watching the punters placing their bets, her perfect scarlet nails resting on the edge of the gaming table and her long, diamanté (or were they real diamond?) earrings flashing white fire as they caught the light from the crystal chandeliers. To Venetia she seemed the embodiment of French sophistication – her glossy red hair twisted up into an impossibly complicated knot, her long black evening dress perfectly simple but sublime on her slender, thoroughbred body.

Venetia knew she was a tolerably good-looking

woman, but she felt positively mousy beside this croupier. She wished she had Cassie's sassy, upfront attitude to life – Cassie could have strolled in here, dressed in jeans and a T-shirt, and nobody would have dared to bat an eyelid.

'*Rien ne va plus*,' announced the croupier. And the wheel spun, black and red merging into a blur as the little ivory ball careered around the rim, to land, at last, in Black 48.

Venetia was about to move on when a figure on the other side of the table caught her eye.

If she had been impressed by the coolly seductive Bastien Le Rocq, she was utterly dumbstruck by the man who was standing opposite, raking in a pile of coloured gaming chips. Their eyes met for a split second, and she felt her senses reeling. There was something about him that compelled her attention, something almost frighteningly magnetic about the attraction she felt for him.

He was one of those agelessly handsome men; maybe thirty-five, maybe older, it was hard to tell. Tall and slim but athletically built, he towered over most of the other gamers standing around the table. His skin was a beautiful light olive colour, his face high-cheekboned and aristocratic, hawk-like and intelligent, his mouth full and sensual. His collar-length hair was raven-black, and as the light caught it it glowed with a blue-black sheen.

But it was his eyes which drew her, and would not let her go. They were like dark, deep coals burning with a secret fire, a cold flame which might kindle into an inferno at the first spark of anger. As he looked back at her, his eyes meeting hers, he did not smile. On the surface he seemed quite uninterested in the blonde Englishwoman in the blue silk dress. But when he turned away, Venetia could still feel the burning of those eyes, could still see the way he had looked at her, the passion of his soul hidden beneath a cold exterior.

As he began to walk away from the table, Venetia nudged Léonore's arm. Léonore swung round.

'What is it, *chérie*?'

'Who is *that*?'

'Who – the blond over there? That's Alain Exupéry, the film star. Isn't he simply irresistible? I know him a little – would you like me to introduce you?'

'No, no, not him. The man over there – the very tall, dark-haired man in the long black jacket.'

Léonore's expression transformed in an instant from girlish excitement to disdain.

'Him?' She gave a dismissive wave of her hand. 'He is nothing. A nobody.'

'But who is he?'

'A professional gambler, a loner. He lives in a villa quite near here, overlooking the sea. I don't know what his full name is. We only know him as

71

Esteban.' She leaned closer to Venetia. 'But if I were you,' *chérie*, I would steer well clear of him. He is arrogant, unpleasant, doesn't mix with the other people around here. He's best left well alone. He's nothing, you understand?'

But as Venetia stared after the tall, dark figure crossing the room to the bar, she couldn't take her eyes off him. Her body ached for him, and in the warm and secret darkness of her soul she longed to know more about the mysterious, fascinating Esteban.

That night, as she lay in her bed at the Villa Le Rocq, Venetia dreamed that she was locked in a golden cage, suspended hundreds of feet above a fathomless, wine-dark sea.

She was not alone in the cage. There was a man with her, standing before her, and his cock was in her mouth. It was a beautiful cock, curved like a sabre, and so huge that she could scarcely take its length between her lips. She could feel the tip pressing against the back of her throat, making it difficult to breathe.

The golden cage swayed over the sea as she sucked at the man's cock. He made no attempt to touch or caress her, but she could feel him hardening as she kissed him, knew the pleasure she was giving him though he gave her no outward sign.

Her hands were bound behind her back, and

she was powerless to do anything but suck on her lover's cock. Yet that was all she wanted to do, for his pleasure was her pleasure. She could smell his desire, hot and musky and urgent. Soon he would spurt. Very, very soon. And she wanted that more than anything else in the world.

His seed astonished her as it spurted into her mouth, for it was cold as ice, chilling and exciting her as it flooded her throat – so abundantly that she could not swallow it, and trickles escaped from her lips, forming thin trails of ice that glittered and shimmered on her skin.

He drew her to her feet and kissed her, and for the first time she saw her lover's face. His diamond-black eyes burned into her, and the trails of ice on her skin began to melt and trickle away, turning to drops of burning-hot water which fell from the cage into the sea below.

They kissed, and as their bodies met, flames began to lick around the ropes which held the cage suspended above the water. In seconds, the ropes were eaten through.

And suddenly, the cage was plummeting towards the water, and she was falling, falling, falling.

Into the arms of Esteban.

Chapter Four

THE OCEAN WATERS were growing colder now, chill fingers lapping greedily at Venetia's bare flesh. And she could feel herself rising up through the many-coloured water, from deep, deep indigo to royal blue; to cobalt and a turquoise green.

The caressing water had explored every nook and niche of Venetia's nakedness, slipping between her thighs to lick at the fringed margin of her sex; sliding across the twin globes of her buttocks; caressing the underside of her buoyant breasts, slipping into the deep valley between and making every inch of her bare flesh tingle.

She had forgotten everything, her mind quite blank and her whole being centred now only on sensations. Who was she? Where was she? Did it really matter? What could be more important than the anticipation of the next silken caress, the next kiss as currents of water thrilled across her swollen nipples?

All she knew as that she was moving upwards, floating and bobbing and rising towards the light. Suddenly she didn't want to rise any higher, because she knew that when she reached the light this would all end. She began to struggle, but the sea had her in its grip, and was dragging her inexorably towards the surface . . .

'*Mon Dieu! Ma petite, qu'est-ce que tu fais ici? Tu veux mourir de froid?*'

'Please . . . let me go . . .'

Hands shook her and Venetia realised, to her chagrin, that she must have been asleep and that all that had passed had been a dream: the golden cage, falling into the deep ocean, Esteban . . .

'Venetia – what on earth are you doing out here in the garden?'

Venetia opened her eyes and found herself looking up into the concerned face of Bastien's cousin, Léonore.

'The garden? But . . .'

She looked down at herself, and realised with a jolt that she was completely naked, lying curled up on a patch of soft, dewy-damp grass and fragrant wild thyme beneath the olive trees in the gardens of the Villa Le Rocq. As she stretched out her limbs and tried to get up, she realised just how long she must have been out here – her muscles were stiff and ached with cold, and her skin was white, clammy and shivery. Goose-pimples ran the length of her arms and legs, and her nipples were as hard and as tough as flower-stalks, though that was perhaps not entirely the result of the cold . . .

Léonore held out her hand and Venetia took it gratefully, using it to lever herself to her feet.

'Don't you remember how you got here?' asked Léonore.

'Nothing. Not a thing. One minute I was in my bed, the next you were waking me up.'

'Do you sleepwalk?'

'Never.'

Léonore felt Venetia's forehead.

'*Tu es malade?*'

'No, no, I'm not ill. I'm fine, just cold. Maybe I heard something and wandered out here. But why would I fall asleep?'

Léonore looked at Venetia, shrugged and burst out laughing.

'*Pauvre* Venetia!' she exclaimed. 'Is our hospitality so lacking that we must drive our guests to spend the night in the garden? Come, Venetia, come back to the house and let me warm you up before you catch your death of cold!'

They walked back up to the house together, Léonore taking off her couture jacket and putting it around Venetia's shoulders. Venetia was struck by how gentle Léonore was towards her, how tender and attentive. And was it her imagination, or was Léonore really trying to find excuses to touch her?

The sensuality of Venetia's dream lingered on inside her like a low flame, waiting to burst back into vibrant, dazzling life. Each step that she took reminded her of the pleasure she had felt in the dream-world of her imagination; for as her thighs moved so her labia rubbed gently together, stimulating the still-swollen bud of her clitoris. She realised, to her slight embarrassment, that she was actually enjoying Léonore's attentions. And her thoughts began to wander, conjuring up pictures she wanted to suppress but couldn't. Pictures of herself, making love with Bastien's cousin Léonore.

She shocked herself with her own sensual creativity. Sex with a woman! The very thought appalled her. Or did it? Since she had come to Valazur in search of Cassie, she scarcely recognised herself or knew what she wanted any more. And Léonore Le Rocq most certainly was a very attractive young woman.

'*Viens*, Venetia.' Léonore pushed open the side door and led Venetia inside. 'Come up to my apartment, *chérie*. You can use my private bathroom.'

'That's very kind, Léonore, but really, there's no need . . .'

'Nonsense.' Léonore's hand was very firmly on her shoulder. It felt good. Surprisingly good. 'Bastien has given me the most extravagant bathroom, and I want you to enjoy it as much as I do.'

That was the end of the argument as far as Léonore was concerned, and Venetia wondered why she'd ever wanted to resist. Why not do exactly as Léonore asked. Why not allow herself to be pampered and preened? It wasn't as if she was accustomed to the easy life. Not like Cassie. Cassie had charmed her way into more high-class hotels and millionaires' beds than Venetia had dug holes in the ground.

They climbed the stairs to the first floor. At this time of the morning, much to Venetia's relief, there were no domestic staff about, no one to see the mad Englishwoman wandering about her host's house, completely naked save for a black couture jacket which scarcely covered the tops of her breasts. She hoped against hope that no one except Léonore had spotted her asleep in Bastien's orange-grove.

Léonore's private apartment was at the back of the villa, with stunning views over the gently wooded hills which rose up above the village of Valazur and sloped down to the sea.

'Here we are, Venetia. Come inside and I shall run you a bath.'

Venetia followed Léonore across a splendid

living-room filled with the finest Scandinavian designer furnishings. These were set off with quirky *objets d'art* – a pair of African tribal statuettes, the female ripe and big-breasted, the male almost menacing with his heavy testicles and hugely erect, conical penis; an exquisite Persian erotic watercolour; a Matisse nude; a set of Egyptian clay *ushabti* figurines. It was obvious that the Le Rocq family didn't only have money – they had taste, too. And a taste for the sensual and the erotic.

On the other side of the living-room a door led through into the bedroom. Venetia had never seen anything quite so sumptuous – it was more like the bedroom of a princess, or perhaps a high-class courtesan, with its heart-shaped bed and satin pillows, its deep-pile carpet and immense wardrobe, the door standing open to reveal row upon row of Versace, Gaultier, Lacroix and Westwood.

Venetia caught sight of herself in the mirror as she walked through into the adjacent bathroom. What a mess she looked! Her blonde hair was tousled and tangled, and full of little bits of twig and leaf. Her skin was patched in places with mud and the greenish tinge of grass stains.

Léonore caught her looking in the mirror and smiled.

'You are a very beautiful woman, *chérie*. Many lovers must have told you that.'

Venetia shivered with silent appreciation. Listening to Léonore's voice was like licking warm honey from a cold, silver teaspoon. How could it do so much to her, make her feel like this? She'd never found women attractive before, and had certainly never wondered what it would be like to have another woman's lips darting kisses over her breasts, her belly, her smooth, rounded buttocks.

'I look dreadful!' she protested.

Léonore's hand stroked sinuously down the long line of Venetia's back and rested on the smooth swell of her backside.

'*Mais non, chérie. Absolument non.* You look . . . divine. But you are cold. I must find a way to make you warm again.'

Venetia could scarcely believe it as she looked into the mirror and saw Léonore bend to plant a kiss upon her shoulder; pushing aside the tangled mass of her hair, pressing her lips against her chilled flesh. Lips that felt so hot, so passionate.

She half-closed her eyes, her body betraying her pleasure with a quiver of response.

'*Chérie,*' breathed Léonore, her voice a soft, smooth whisper in Venetia's ear. 'Come with me.'

Venetia responded instinctively, following Léonore into the bathroom. It was as grand as a classical temple, the walls and floor lined with white marble and marble pillars stretching from floor to ceiling. Luxuriant plants wound their way about the pillars, brilliant green tendrils and shady leaves lending a tropical feel to the room.

The room was lit with natural light, the ceiling sloping like an artist's studio, so that half of the ceiling and almost the whole of one wall formed an immense window. This was decorated with swirling patterns in stained glass – reds and yellows and pastel shades of green and blue forming a filter for the soft morning light and casting pools of luminescent colour on the white marble floor.

To one side of the bathroom was a sunken bath – but not just any sunken bath. This was a huge and luxurious Jacuzzi; a wide, sweeping oval of pink-veined marble, deep enough to wallow in up to the neck, big enough for two . . . or three, or more.

Léonore turned on the taps and hot water began thundering into the bath. She added drops of scented oil from a tiny blue glass bottle, selected from a shelf filled with every imaginable luxury.

'It is my own special blend of essential oils,' explained Léonore, picking up a brush and beginning to tease the tangles from Venetia's hair. 'This part of France is rich in aromatic plants and flowers. I gather them to make my own cosmetics and massage oils.'

Venetia relaxed at Léonore's touch. It was rather like being a small girl again, but Venetia didn't mind. It was so soothing, feeling the brush move slowly through her hair, the soft bristles massaging her scalp. No not a child: a pet animal. It was like being a kitten, stroked so gently and so skilfully that it made her want to purr with pleasure.

'Mmm. It smells lovely,' said Venetia, breathing in the waft of sweetness which rose from the water.

'What can you smell?'

'Lavender, rosemary I think . . . and something musky – is it cinnamon? And roses, and . . . oh, I can't tell. Just when I think I know what it is, it seems to change!'

Léonore laughed pleasantly. 'It is a secret,' she told Venetia. 'My secret recipe. There are twenty different flower-oils and herbal essences in it, you know – and other ingredients, too, little tricks my mother taught me to relax the body.' She laid down the hairbrush, scraped back Venetia's long mass of blonde hair and secured it in a knot. Her fingers slid down the nape of Venetia's neck and rested on her shoulders, stroking the flesh. 'You are very tense, *ma chérie*. Would you like me to relax you?'

'I . . .'

'*Mas bien sûr*, of course you would, my dear.'

Léonore's fingers began kneading and squeezing Venetia's shoulders. Venetia winced. Léonore was right, of course – her shoulder-muscles had acquired all the inflexibility of steel cables after a night spent curled into an awkward position on the grass. And Léonore seemed to know all the tricks, all the little knacks to ease away the tension. At first, her caresses were quite painful, bringing the discomfort to the surface and, as if by magic, making it simply evaporate.

'Mmm . . . that feels good. Wherever did you learn to do that?'

'Massage is not something one learns, *chérie*. It is an instinct – a natural gift, if you like.' Léonore's lips touched the flesh she had reddened with her rough caresses. 'I'm sure you have the gift too, Venetia. The gift of giving pleasure with your fingers.'

'I . . . don't know what you mean,' gasped Venetia, as Léonore's right hand slid down from her shoulder and cradled the heavy globe of her breast.

'Non, chérie. No, perhaps you do not. Not yet. But if you will only let me show you . . .'

Her fingers closed about the breast, Venetia's nipple poking out between middle and fourth finger, the gap closing gradually until the fingers were tight about the fleshy stalk, rubbing hard as Léonore's hand began to make slow, circular movements.

'Oh! Oh Léonore . . .!' Venetia's cry was part astonishment, part shame, part excitement . . . oh, and how exciting it felt to experience these first caresses from a woman, awakening lusts she had never dreamed that she could have inside her woman's body.

'Good, *chérie*?'

'Good. Oh Léonore, it feels *really* good.'

'Relax, Venetia. Let the tensions melt away. That's it, *chérie*. Don't fight it. That's it . . .'

Léonore's left hand slipped down to cup Venetia's other breast. The combined effect of her caresses was far greater than their individual erotogenic power. Léonore was still fully dressed, yet, Venetia could feel her desire. Her nipples were hard and were pushing against the thin fabric of her summer blouse, grinding into Venetia's bare back. Her breath was hot and spicy on her cheek. Her belly was pressing against Venetia's backside, her hips tilting in a long, slow dance of desire.

'I want you, Venetia,' she whispered. 'I've wanted to have you since the moment Bastien brought you back to the villa.'

'But Léonore . . . you don't understand. I've never . . .'

Léonore turned her protests to moans of pleasure with a long line of kisses, beginning behind her ear and running down her neck, her shoulder, between her shoulder-blades. And all the time, her hands were cupping Venetia's breasts, slowly moving, awakening levels of desire which had existed so deep within her that she had never even suspected their existence.

'Of course I understand, *chérie*. I am exactly the same as you. I love men, but I love women too. Why should we confine ourselves only to making love with men? Think of it . . . exploring your sexuality with someone who understands your body completely, because her body is so very much like yours.'

'Please . . .' Venetia's pleading whisper shook her entire body. She was close to tears, her head reeling and her body responding even though her mind was screaming, no, no, no.

Yes . . . whispered her body. Yes, do it. You know how good it will feel. Cassie would do it. Cassie wouldn't be afraid. You aren't afraid are you, Venetia?

'Come into the bath, Venetia. You are cold. The warm water will make you feel much, much better. I promise I won't do anything you don't want me to do.'

As Léonore's hand stroked her backside, Venetia knew her resistance as all play-acting, a complete sham for the benefit of these last vestiges of her modesty. And what was the point in playing the blushing virgin, if what you really were, deep down, was a hot and passionate slut, simply longing to learn all the secrets of pleasure that you had denied yourself for too, too long?

She climbed into the bath, gasping as the hot water lapped its way up her ankles, her calves, her thighs . . . and then oozed and swirled between her thighs, its prurient tongue seeking out the very heart of her shameless need.

Venetia watched as Léonore undressed before her. She seemed completely unselfconscious about taking her clothes off in front of another woman – almost a complete stranger. Under the blouse and chic, thigh-length skirt, she was wearing a full slip in écru silk, its slender straps already sliding down over her arms, revealing the bare expanse of shoulder and breast beneath.

She pulled the slip off over her head, and Venetia saw how pert and round and hard her breasts were – just like small apples, bursting with sweet juice. They were tanned the same amber-gold as the rest of her body, the nipples brown as chocolate drops and equally tempting. Unfastening the side button of her French knickers, Léonore let them slide down to her ankles, then stepped out of them, kicking them contemptuously aside.

Underneath, she was perfectly bare; her pubis shaven so that, with her small breasts and lean, athletic figure, Léonore might have passed for a pubescent girl. Even that thought excited Venetia, and for a fleeting instant she imagined that they were schoolgirls together, exploring each other's bodies for the first time, unwittingly discovering the hidden truths of their sex.

Léonore slid into the water beside her, and as she did so the fragrant waves lapped up around

Venetia's breasts, making them float like pink-white clouds upon the scented water, the nipples deepening to the dusky pink of unopened rosebuds.

Léonore shook the pins from her hair, and let it tumble down into the warm water, floating out behind her like a raft of russet-coloured sea-wrack. Venetia reached out and twisted a tendril of hair about her finger. It felt springy, lithe, full of energy just like Léonore herself. Full of a dangerous electricity . . .

'Can you feel the oil soothing you, *ma chérie*?' Léonore stroked her fingers down Venetia's shoulder and then, beneath the water, over the curves of her backside.

'Mmm, yes . . . it's making me quite dizzy.' Venetia's head was swimming, very pleasantly, almost as if she had drunk a whole bottle of wine and was floating in a delicate mist of intoxication.

'And is it making you more . . . relaxed?' Léonore's hands were on Venetia's hips now, smoothing and caressing. 'Does it make you want to *fuck* me, *chère* Venetia?'

The deliberate emphasis which Léonore used gave the word even more impact than it would otherwise have had. Venetia found herself gazing straight into Léonore's green eyes, magnetised by that sensual yet insistent gaze. For long moments they simply looked at each other in silence, Venetia's body singing with joy at Léonore's sly caresses. And then, all of a sudden, the words came tumbling out.

'I . . . I feel . . . sexy, excited, aroused . . . oh, I can't describe it, Léonore . . .'

'But it feels good, *oui*?'

Venetia felt her whole body simultaneously tensing and relaxing. 'It feels indecently good.'

'Let me show you what to do to give a woman pleasure, Venetia.' Léonore reached out and took a brand-new cake of creamy white soap from the dish beside the bath. It was an exfoliating soap, pitted with little flakes of oatmeal designed to abrade the skin lightly and remove the dead cells. But Léonore had a different use for it.

She lathered up the bar of soap and ran it first over Venetia's shoulders and upper arms, then over the generous swell of her breasts, holding each breast in turn, and rubbing the soap quite hard over the bare skin.

Venetia shrieked her protest, but Léonore held her fast – and besides, the last thing Venetia wanted was for this to stop. It was as if she had stepped straight back into her dream; only this time, everything in it was real.

'You see, *ma chérie*? You see how good it feels to have the roughness of the soap rubbing over and over your breasts? I have a friend, in Paris – it excites her to have me rub sandpaper over her nipples. But I am gentler with you, *n'est-ce pas*, Venetia? I am not such a cruel mistress.'

She rinsed the soap-suds off Venetia's breasts, sending little runnels of soapy water coursing down over the full, firm globes and melting into the warm, rose-tinged water. Venetia felt almost a sense of regret as Léonore handed her the bar of soap, for her clitoris was aching and burning, and with each new caress as the water filtered between her outer labia, her desire was becoming a desperate, feverish need.

'Why don't you pleasure me, Venetia? See if you can make me come.' She smiled, and kissed Venetia very passionately, full on the lips. *'Pauvre enfant.* You make me want to come so very much. You make me wish I was a man, so I could fuck you with my big, hard dick. You'd like that, wouldn't you?'

Venetia did not reply, but in her mind she was imagining it: Léonore as she was now – powerfully feminine yet boyishly athletic – and then as she might be, an hermaphrodite creature with a huge, curving penis which stabbed into her like a sabre. She felt a new wetness between her thighs – not just the fragrant, oily water in the bath, but another fragrance, a new elixir, trickling from the well-spring of her sex. How could she not have realised how much it excited her to think of having sex with a woman? How could she not have realised how much she desired Léonore Le Rocq?

'You know I would,' she replied. And this time

it was Venetia who kissed Léonore, her tongue parting the French woman's lips, darting into her mouth, possessing her as a man posseses a woman, fucking her with her tongue.

The waters splashed about them as they embraced, thigh between thigh, breast against breast. And then Venetia pulled away, gasping, dizzy with the exhilaration of this wicked, forbidden desire which she had at last begun to express.

'Now take me,' said Léonore. She did not beg. She knew she did not need to. Venetia was already the slave of her own passion. 'Fuck me, Venetia. Show me how you want me to give pleasure to you. Show me now.'

Venetia's grip tightened on the bar of soap. It felt at once slippery and rough in her palm. Slowly and with immense enjoyment, she began rubbing it over and over Léonore's apple-hard breasts.

'*Ah oui, chérie, tu as le diable aux doigts*, do it harder, harder, yes, yes!'

As astonished by her own excitement as by Léonore's, Venetia began to stimulate the French woman's body with a new ardour. A fire seemed to course through her own loins as she moved the soap-bar down, down, below the water-line.

It rubbed over Léonore's buttocks with a satisfying scratchiness, clouds of white, foamy lather floating away from the smooth, tanned skin and clouding the water. She hesitated for a moment, and then, feeling Léonore parting her thighs in the sweetly-scented water, she slipped the soap between her buttocks.

At the first touch of the soap in her most intimate furrow, Léonore let out a shrill squeal of pleasure, her eyes wide with surprised pleasure, her mouth forming a tight O of wordless ecstasy.

To Venetia, it felt almost as though everything she was doing to Léonore, she was doing to herself. In her imagination she could feel the rough soap rubbing over her own tight brown anus, felt it puckering, alternately dilating and contracting, welcoming in the shameless invader.

And then, emboldened, she slid the soap down, down, down still further, moving from the amber rose of Léonore's anus to the soft pink sea-anemone of her sex, whose mouth opened wide in a glistening coral kiss of welcome.

'Chérie, ah oui! Chérie . . .'

Venetia was hardly listening to Léonore's groans and sighs of pleasure, only to the rhythmic thumping of her own heart, the blood in her veins, pumping and surging, the regular pulsing of her own, neglected clitoris. She thrust the bar of soap into Léonore's slippery-wet sex with a single, smooth movement.

Léonore's whole body went rigid, her arms thrashing the water as the welter of sensations overtook her, the smoothness of the soap and the roughness of the grains of oatmeal, abrading the soft, wet tunnel of her sex. Léonore's sex-muscles seized it and held it within her, clenching about it, even though the effort must have been both agonisingly uncomfortable and so, so arousing.

Venetia slipped her thigh between Léonore's leg and pushed it up hard against the French girl's labia. The hardness of muscled thigh and the hardness of Léonore's pubic bone met across soft flesh, Léonore's sexual wetness oozing out of her and smearing Venetia's thigh before dissolving into the surrounding water.

Was there something in this water, besides the oil? Or did the oil itself embody some uniquely aphrodisiac quality? Venetia hardly knew what she was doing, but she knew how good it felt to have a woman's pleasure in her hands, on her lips, her thigh.

Léonore came with a piercing shriek of pleasure, her hands clutching at Venetia so convulsively that she almost pulled her under the water.

'*Diable!*' gasped Léonore, slumping against Venetia's shoulder as the last of her pleasure ebbed away. 'There is such power in your caresses.'

Venetia shared her kisses, accepting them with a fervour she would have thought impossible a day or even an hour before. And then, quite suddenly, the tables were turned and it was

Léonore who was taking the offensive in this war of lust.

She pushed Venetia back against the side of the bath, kissing and biting her, rubbing her pubis with jerky, feverish movements which drove Venetia to the very brink of insanity.

'Now,' she gasped. 'Now I must show you the pleasure that one woman can give another. Sit on the edge of the bath and part your thighs for me, *chérie*.'

Venetia did as she was bidden, desperate for Léonore's fingers to explore the inner sanctum of her sex, to give her the release that she had longed for since the moment she awoke in the garden, still a prisoner of her own erotic dreams.

But it was not Léonore's fingers which found their way into Venetia's sex. Reaching for the shower-head, Léonore switched on the water, turning up higher and higher until dozens of powerful jets were spurting from its tip.

Her fingers parted Venetia's plump, sex-swollen labia and Venetia struggled briefly, afraid of what was going to happen next. Only there could be no escape – for she was utterly enslaved to her own desire. And when the tiny, needle-sharp jets of water assailed her throbbing clitoris, she knew that ecstasy could not be long in coming.

It was almost lunchtime when Venetia and

Léonore came downstairs – washed, dressed and neither of them mentioning one word of what had gone before. No one would have suspected the pleasure which they had just shared in Léonore's bathroom.

Joseph, Bastien's valet, had left them a light lunch of salad, cheese and wine, and they took it on to the patio at the back of the villa. Léonore switched on the local television station.

'And now, the local news.' A picture flashed up on the screen, and Venetia almost dropped her wine-glass on the floor.

'Is something the matter, *chérie*?'

'Sh, please, Léonore . . .'

Venetia listened intently, her eyes widening with horror as the details unfolded. An English journalist had been found dead on the beach near Valazur that very morning. Murdered. The corpse of an Englishman with a severed throat, drained of its life-force, as bloodless as a side of pork.

An Englishman called Evan Peterson.

'My God!' exclaimed Venetia, clapping her hands to her face.

'*Chérie*? What is the matter?'

'I . . . I knew him. Or at least, I met him once.'

Léonore shrugged. '*Tant pis*. But he was a journalist, *non*? Journalists make many enemies. Perhaps he asked too many questions.'

Venetia wasn't listening. She was looking at the screen, at pictures taken at the spot where the body had been found. There it was, a shapeless mass lying under a blanket; a few people standing around, one or two walking in the background, bored gendarmes . . .

'Léonore?'

'*Oui?*'

'That man – the one standing at the back, the distinguished-looking one with the greying hair. I've seen him before, in Gérard's bar. Do you know him?'

She thought back to that first day, to when she'd looked across the bar to see a man watching her as he stroked a beautiful woman's thigh. Watching her as though he fully intended to possess her.

'*Hein . . . oui, bien sûr.* Everyone around Valazur knows him.'

'Then tell me . . . who is he?'

'That is Jean-Marc Levigny, Venetia. A local wine-grower. He and Cassie were quite close, actually. They had a hot affair. You know, I think Bastien was quite jealous!'

Really, thought Venetia to herself as the reporter moved on to the next story. Then you and I had better have a little chat, Monsieur Jean-Marc Levigny.

It was a long day, and when at last night came, Venetia was glad for a chance to crawl into bed and try to shut out the thoughts which teemed like a million insects inside her brain.

But her thoughts were not so easy to suppress, or to censor. Whatever had she thought she was doing, having sex with Léonore Le Rocq? Had she completely taken leave of her senses? And then there were the new and disturbing complications which the day had brought. Who had killed Evan Peterson, and could his death be in any way connected to Cassie's disappearance? And what – if anything – did Monsieur Jean-Marc Levigny have to do with it all?

She lay awake in the sultry night, unable to sleep, listening to the frogs croaking in the undergrowth and the rattle of the dry branches tap, tap, tapping against her window.

The woman's scream cut through the stillness of the night like fingernails scraping across a wet blackboard. In an instant Venetia was on her feet, slipping on her dressing-gown and slippers.

There was only one other person in the house tonight, and that was Léonore.

Venetia hurried down the corridor, as fast as she could in the darkness, which was broken only by occasional patches of moonlight. She dared not put on the light – if there really was an intruder, it could be dangerous to advertise her presence here. But she must do something to find out what was happening to Léonore.

She climbed the last few stairs and found herself outside the door of Léonore's apartment. Silence. Nothing. Could she possible have been mistaken?

And then another scream broke the silence; a third and a fourth, strangely staccato and curtailed. Gathering together all her courage, Venetia turned the door-handle. Inside, the sitting-room was in darkness, but she could see light filtering through the half-closed door to the bedroom.

Seizing one of the African statuettes, Venetia crept across the room towards the bedroom door. It seemed like the furthest she had ever had to travel, and she was convinced that at any moment a creaking floorboard would give her away.

'Aah, aah, aah!'

The sound was louder, shriller still as Venetia approached the bedroom door. Should she go in? No, of course she shouldn't – she didn't have a death wish and besides, she wouldn't be much use to Venetia unconscious or dead.

She slid into the shadows beside the door, hoping against hope that her own shadow would not give her away. And, pressing her face very close against the door-frame, she peered through the two or three inches of light into the room beyond.

What she saw astonished her. It was indeed Léonore who was crying out . . . but not in pain. She was bending over the end of the heart-shaped bed, her black satin nightdress hanging down from her waist, and her back and breasts completely bare and criss-crossed with lurid red stripes.

Someone was standing behind her, and as she watched, round-eyed with alarm, Venetia saw a riding-crop fall onto the already reddened flesh at Léonore's back. A few droplets of blood had welled up into fat crimson beads, where the crop had cut through the skin, and a single red trickle ran from between her shoulder-blades to the base of her spine.

'Ah! Ah, *ayez pitié* . . .'

Her cries for mercy were perhaps heeded, for Venetia saw the riding-crop fall to the ground as a figure walked towards the bed, stepping out of the shadows.

Venetia drew in breath, scarcely able to prevent herself crying out. Jean-Marc Levigny? No, it couldn't be . . . could it? To hear Léonore talk, you'd have thought they were scarcely more than acquaintances. And Venetia cast her mind back to that afternoon, to the incongruity of a dead man on a sunny beach, surrounded by ghoulish onlookers. Onlookers who had included Jean-Marc Levigny.

She knew that she had not been mistaken. It could not be anyone but Levigny – that greying hair, that muscular frame, that rugged profile. And she remembered those broad, strong hands, smoothing over his companion's thigh; his pale eyes gazing at her, devouring her, demanding her surrender.

Heart pounding so loudly that she was sure he must be able to hear it, she watched with reluctant fascination as Levigny unzipped his flies and took out his penis.

It seemed to glisten like polished glass in the glow from the pink-shaded wall-lights which surrounded the bed. There was something machine-like, mechanistic, about this expressionless man, slowly stripping the silk slip from Léonore's backside, baring the firm, tanned flesh beneath.

Venetia watched as he began to masturbate over Léonore's upraised backside, his hand moving very slowly and very luxuriously on his shaft, his eyes fixed on the quivering gloves of flesh, the purple head of his cock alternately covered and uncovered by his foreskin.

It was like watching something out of some bizarre silent film. When Levigny climaxed, even his seed seemed to spurt out of him in slow-motion, landing in thick, pearly gobbets all over Léonore's back and backside.

And as Levigny bent forward to lick his seed from Léonore's buttocks, Venetia felt the strangest tumult of sensations overwhelming her.

A seductive mélange of arousal and dread.

Chapter Five

THE NEXT TIME Venetia visited the casino, she found an excuse to go alone. After what she had seen through Léonore's bedroom door, she no longer felt at ease with Bastien's cousin.

Was it possible that Léonore and Jean-Marc had had something to do with Cassie's disappearance? And did they know more about the death of Evan Peterson than Léonore was prepared to admit? Such thoughts troubled Venetia, and she longed to come right out and ask Léonore what she knew. But what if her fears proved well-founded? What then? No, she would have to move carefully, get her information little by little without betraying her suspicions.

She was going to begin with Jean-Marc

Levigny. That was why she had decided on the casino. Léonore had let slip that Levigny adored blackjack and roulette, and if Venetia just happened to bump into him, why shouldn't an English tourist visit the local casino for a night of glamour and glitz?

Venetia caught sight of her reflection in a tall mirror as she walked through the lobby and handed her wrap to the girl in the cloakroom. The dress she had borrowed from Léonore had made a striking difference to her appearance, so much so that she had to take a second look before she could accept that the woman in the mirror really was herself.

Her reflection gazed calmly back at her, chic, sophisticated, even sultry. Venetia had piled up her honey-blonde hair into loosely pinned curls, leaving just two or three long, wavy tendrils to kiss the back of her bare neck and shoulders.

The dress was an electric blue satin which brought out the blue in her eyes. The body-hugging skirt was pencil-slim, hugging her hips and belly and falling to a sequinned hem, just above her ankles. As she moved, the skirt fell open at a deep split which ran from upper thigh to ankle, baring the whole of one long, slender leg – which looked longer still because of the outrageously high-heeled shoes which Léonore had persuaded her to buy in Nice.

The top half of the dress struggled to contain

her ample breasts. After all, the dress had been designed and tailored to fit Léonore and, while they were more or less the same height and build, Venetia's breasts were a good deal fuller. The tightly-boned, strapless bodice held her in a vice-like embrace, pushing up her breasts so that they seemed indecently large, their ripe swell almost spilling over the edge of the fitted bodice.

About her neck she wore a simple choker of deep-blue velvet ribbon, on to which she had pinned her only valuable item of jewellery – the diamond brooch she had been left by her great-aunt. It wasn't ostentatious – not like some of the things she had seen rich women wearing around clubs in the Riviera resorts – but it added a touch of sparkle to an already glamorous outfit.

Tucking her evening bag under her arm, she walked through into the main gaming room.

'Bonsoir, madame. Du champagne?'

Venetia accepted a glass from the silver tray and walked towards the blackjack table, mingling with the crowd of casual observers. She was sure for one moment that she had spotted Jean-Marc Levigny, but when the man turned round she saw that it was a stranger. She must try to be less jumpy. After all, she might be imagining the whole thing. It would be typical of Cassie to waltz off to Rio with some rich hunk and completely forget to tell anyone where she was going.

Then she saw him. He was standing on the

other side of the room, one elbow resting on the massive carved fireplace, the other hand holding a champagne flute. A heap of coloured gaming chips lay on the mantelpiece beside him, but his eyes were not on the gaming tables. They were on Venetia.

A thrill of sudden, unwilling excitement ran through Venetia as her eyes met his.

Esteban.

He was dressed in a long, black, fitted jacket and trousers that were almost Edwardian in their tailoring, a waistcoat of crimson embroidered silk, and a crisp white shirt with a wing-collar. A knotted silk cravat and cufflinks of polished jet completed the effect of immaculate decadence, of the bored dandy obsessed by his own beauty.

And he *was* beautiful – or at least, utterly compelling. His jet-black, wavy hair was pushed back from an almost gaunt, hawkish face which was striking rather than handsome, but which drew the eye to dark eyes and finely sculpted, sensual lips.

For some reason, she knew not why, Venetia found herself walking towards him across the crowded room, everything else around her fading into insignificance, thoughts of Jean-Marc Levigny pushed far to the back of her mind.

She needed to talk to Esteban. There was something about him . . . something she couldn't define but which compelled attention. His dark eyes, cold and fiery as black diamonds, seemed to draw her to him, glittering and seductive. She must talk to him.

'*Monsieur?*'

Esteban feigned to have just noticed her. He did not smile.

'*Mademoiselle?*' His voice was deep, dark, curiously soft and caressing beneath a thin veneer of superiority.

'I . . . I was hoping we could talk. You don't know me, but my name is Venetia. Venetia Fellowes.'

Esteban's aristocratic features relaxed slightly as the corners of his mouth twitched, resisting the weakness of a smile.

'I know you, Mademoiselle Fellowes.' He sipped his drink, still looking into Venetia's eyes. 'Your sister was a very foolish young woman.'

Venetia caught her breath. This man was utterly infuriating, he made her want to hit him, with his mocking half-smiles and his air of superiority. But there was more to it than that, something deeper and far less superficial. Something that awoke echoes of desire inside Venetia, made her want to undress slowly for him, to beg him to let her kiss the slumbering serpent of his penis . . .

'You knew my sister, *Monsieur* . . .?'

'Esteban. You may call me Esteban.' He sat his glass down on the mantelpiece. 'I knew Cassan-

104

dra . . . a little. We met, but she was silly and superficial, she did not interest me.'

Venetia fought down the tide of anger within her. It really wouldn't do to lose her temper and thump Esteban, even if he was – as Léonore had claimed – a 'nobody'.

'Really?' she forced herself to ask with an icy calmness.

Esteban gave a grim laugh.

'Really, Mademoiselle Fellowes. You are much too naive. You see, Venetia, in my life I have known many women and most of them have been exactly like your sister – empty-headed creatures with no virtue but their beauty.'

He stretched out his right hand and stroked Venetia's cheek. His fingertips felt oddly cool on this sultry July night. Venetia caught his hand and prised it away from her face, though her body was crying out for his touch.

'You do not admire beauty, Esteban?'

Esteban's eyes travelled slowly around the room, over pretty women in low-cut dresses and handsome men, their bodies muscular and full of life.

'Beauty fades, Venetia. In time you will come to know that.'

Venetia found his words strangely chilling. What *was* it with this maddening man? She searched for another way to strike up a conversation.

'Have you lived in Valazur for long?' she enquired.

Esteban ran his hand through his hair. It was thick, glossy; and kissable, like those surprisingly sensual lips.

'Does it matter?'

'I . . . No.' And of course it didn't, not really; only Venetia had this funny feeling that it might.

Esteban's eyes glittered. She could see that he was enjoying tormenting her like this, as a cat enjoys playing with a mouse before finally severing its neck with a single bite.

'Why are you interested in me, Venetia?'

'Because . . . because you knew Cassie.'

'But I have told you. Cassandra was just another young woman, perfectly unremarkable.'

A shiver of fear ran down Venetia's spine.

'*Was?* You keep saying "was".'

'Do I?'

'What do you know about Cassie? Do you know what's happened to her?' Venetia heard her voice getting louder, and when she stopped speaking she saw that a few heads had turned in her direction.

Esteban laid a hand on her shoulder. She was furious with him, a little afraid of him too, and she wanted to push him away, to ask him who the hell he thought he was. Only that wasn't what she really wanted, was it? What she really wanted was for Esteban to touch and go on touching her.

106

'Why should I know anything about your sister's disappearance?'

'But you said . . .'

'I was merely making an assumption.' Cool as ice, Esteban took a sip of champagne. 'A perfectly reasonable assumption, given that your sister disappeared in the middle of the night several weeks ago and has never returned.'

'You couldn't give a damn, could you? All you care about is your gambling.'

Esteban shrugged.

'I have long since ceased to care about anyone or anything, Venetia. You would do well to remember that.' He paused. 'But I have a few words of advice for you, *ma jolie petite anglaise*. It would profit you to heed them.'

'Why would you want to give me advice?'

His touch on her bare shoulder thrilled her, sent frissons of cold, terrifying pleasure through her body, made her nipples turn to stone beneath the boned satin of her dress. There was so much desperate, violent wanting in her that she could scarcely bear it. Surely he must be able to feel her hunger, vibrating at the touch of his hand?

The dark smoothness of his voice made her clitoris throb and tingle with suppressed hunger.

'Because you amuse me, *petite anglaise*. Because you have a certain . . . spirit. Listen to me.' He gripped her shoulder harder. 'There are dangers in Valazur, Venetia.'

'Meaning?'

'Meaning nothing. Meaning only that it would be regrettable if you were also to disappear. Perhaps it would be safer if you were to return home to England. Immediately.'

'I am staying here until I find out exactly what has happened to my sister,' replied Venetia defiantly.

Esteban gave a curt nod.

'It is your own choice.' He turned and started walking away.

'And is that all the advice you can give me?' demanded Venetia to his receding back.

He turned and looked at her over his shoulder. Oh, but he was beautiful. Beautiful enough to make a woman lose her mind over him, cold enough to drive her insane with frustrated desire.

'It was a pity about Peterson,' he observed, his face expressionless but his eyes menacingly bright. 'Particularly since he never did manage to publish that article he was researching. But journalists make notes, do they not? If you insist in pursuing this insane quest, perhaps you should visit his apartment.'

'But where . . .?'

'That is for you to find out in any way you can, Mademoiselle Venetia,' replied Esteban. 'I have told you all I know. Now leave me. I have a living to earn.'

She watched him walk away, tall, confident,

somehow detached from the glamorous world around him and yet irresistibly glamorous himself. She didn't trust him – how could she? She didn't even like him.

But she wanted him. Oh, how she wanted him. Her body ached to feel his caresses on her naked, willing flesh.

It took two days of probing and prying to find out the exact location of Evan Peterson's apartment.

Even when she had the address in her hand, Venetia wondered if doing this was a good idea. After all, why should she take any notice of anything a man like Esteban told her? He'd made it perfectly clear he had no interest in Cassie's disappearance, and it had frightened her, the way he had been able to make here feel with just a look, a touch.

And yet . . . she'd felt that there was something more behind the empty words, the mocking smile. For a few, fleeting seconds she had even thought that he desired her as much as she desired him. But that was madness. All Esteban cared about was his own self-importance.

Still, here she was. She took the slip of paper out of her shorts pocket and glanced at it. *Apartment 2, 15 rue Marcel Pagnol, Cap Carlotte.*

In the week or so since Peterson's bloodless corpse had been found on the beach, the local gendarmerie had gone through the motions of investigating the case, but seemed to have lost interest remarkably quickly. What was more, it was almost impossible to get the locals to talk about the murder – although one night, in Gérard's bar, she had overheard someone saying that this wasn't the first bizarre killing in the area over the years. Just what the hell was going on? Maybe she would find some of the answers in Peterson's flat – or then again, maybe Esteban had just been playing games with her.

Peterson's apartment was on the ground floor of an old converted bakery, and even for an amateur burglar like Venetia it wasn't exactly difficult to break in. The difficult thing was in making sure she wasn't spotted.

The window-catch yielded surprisingly easily, and she climbed in over the ledge, jumping down into the kitchen and closing the window behind her.

The apartment seemed to be exactly as Peterson had left it. Walking through into the living-room, Venetia was struck by its sheer ordinariness. A copy of *France-Soir* lay open on the table, next to a cup of coffee with green fur on the surface. Pens, pencils, a GameBoy, rolled-up socks and empty wine-bottles – it could have been a bachelor flat just about anywhere in the world.

Just exactly where to look, that was Venetia's problem. She dared not spend too long here, in case someone noticed her moving around and called the police. Now *that* would be difficult to explain away. She slid open drawers, finding most of them empty or filled with the jumble of old bits and pieces you find in every furnished, rented flat.

It wasn't until she went into Peterson's bedroom that she found what she was looking for. Hell, she didn't even know what she was looking for until it was in her hand.

She'd looked in all the usual places – the drawers, the wardrobe, in the suitcases under the bed. But something prompted her to sit down in the battered old armchair by the bed, and immediately she felt something hard and angular under the seat-cushion. Lifting it up, she found a hard-backed book.

Peterson's diary.

Feverishly, she began leafing through it. Dates, people, meetings in places she'd never even heard of – it was inconsequential and deeply uninteresting. Disappointed, she flicked through the remainder of the pages half-heartedly, and several sheets of folded paper fluttered out.

She picked them up, unfolded them and began reading, shockwaves coursing through her as she scanned Peterson's notes.

May 12. Brasserie Gérard. I'm sure Levigny is up to something but I don't want to push too hard or he'll cotton on. There's danger here, I know there is.

Went to the public archives, talked myself in. There have been ten of these really weird killings over the last fifty years! Not to mention the recent disappearance – young women mostly.

June 1. Still no sign of the Fellowes girl. They've got her, I'm sure of it. But who are they? I can't be certain but I think there's some sort of bizarre cult activity going on around here. Levigny's in it, for sure. Maybe Inspector Defarge too, so I'll need to be careful what I say to the cops. God knows who else. Don't know about religion though – sex seems to be the main thing about all this.

July 3. I'm really scared now. I saw it. I followed Levigny and I saw what goes on. They meet in this underground room – it's dark and the smell of incense makes you dizzy. The smell of sex, too. Oh God, it was terrible but it made me so hard, just watching what they did to that girl. I was touching myself, I can't believe I did that now, but it's true. I had my hand on my cock and I was masturbating while I watched Levigny and the other tying the girl down.

She was writhing and moaning on the stone slab. I don't think she was crying out with pain . . . they'd given her something, and her nipples were hard as iron. Her legs were wide apart, and I could see all the juice trickling out of her. She was so excited.

But not as excited as I was. God help me, I was so

out of my head I didn't even remember to switch on the tape recorder. They were doing these terrible things and all I was doing was rubbing my cock, spurting my jism all over the floor whilst Levigny was licking his out of the girl's pussy. I'll have to do this all over again, get some evidence I can really use.

July 10. Tried to warn Venetia Fellowes, but she wasn't having any of it. Thinks I'm a pervert, I think. I have to do something to make her realise the danger she's in.

July 15. They are meeting tonight. I overheard them talking. I'm afraid, but I have to go there.'

That was the last entry. As Venetia stared at the sheet of paper, dumbstruck, she realised why.

On the morning of July 16, Evan Peterson had been found murdered.

Esteban's villa was set apart from the village; an old, craggy structure on the top of a hill overlooking the sea.

As Venetia drove the borrowed Citroën up the coast road towards the house, its dark shape silhouetted against the deepening royal blue of the evening sky, she wondered if this was going to turn out to be the stupidest thing she'd ever done.

The contents of Peterson's notes had left her feeling jumpy, to say the least. So she'd been right about Levigny . . . but Defarge? The local police inspector? Surely that couldn't be true. And what was all this about some sexy cult?

Why was she coming to see Esteban? What strange force had drawn her here, away from the safe cosiness of Bastien's villa? Or was it safe? She couldn't even be sure about that any more. Maybe Esteban was right. Maybe she should turn tail and get the hell out of Valazur. But she couldn't let Cassie down, and she damn well wasn't going to, no matter what Esteban might have to say about it.

Esteban. The very thought of him filled her with a terrible, aching desire which simply would not go away. The erotic dream she had had about him had been only the beginning. Then there had been her meeting with him at the casino, the fire and ice of his touch leaving her fearful but yearning for more. Now she could not get him out of her mind, thoughts of him filling her whole being. She had thought her attraction to Ramon and Bastien was strong and impetuous; but now she was discovering the true meaning of sexual hunger.

It gnawed at her belly, swelled her labia, turned her clitoris to a hard, juicy rosebud which longed to blossom. As the car bounced over the bumpy road, she felt the vibrations torturing her, jolting her sex and making her stiff nipples jiggle tormentingly inside the lacy cups of her bra. The matching white lace panties she was wearing were already moist with the oozings of her sex, and as her backside moved across the seat, the gusset pushed its way between the lobes of her sex, pressing with unbearable precision against the very heart of her need.

She slowed down as the gates to Esteban's villa came into view. To her surprise they swung open at her approach, and she drove straight on to the long, winding drive which led to the house on the hill.

It was a rather peculiar old house – not especially large or ostentatious, like many of the villas around here (the Villa Le Rocq in particular) – but stylish in a rather Gothic way. It was built from a honey-yellow stone which had weathered and faded a little over the years, but which still glowed in sun or moonlight. There were turrets and towers, and a small lodge with a stone arch leading to the front of the house. It was just like a miniature château.

Venetia parked the car outside the front steps and started walking towards the door. Her heart was thumping, her mind reeling. She had forgotten every single word she had meant to say.

Hesitantly, she rang the doorbell.

It seemed as though a thousand years passed before at last she heard footsteps and the door opened. To her surprise, it was not a servant who opened the door, but Esteban himself, more sardonically good-looking than ever.

They observed each other in silence for a few moments, Venetia struck dumb by the realisation of her own vulnerability, her utter helplessness in the face of this darkly handsome man.

'I have been expecting you,' announced Esteban.

'But how . . .?'

'You had better come in.'

He stepped back to let her in and she brushed against him as she walked into the dimly lit hallway. There were no electric lights along the passageway, only oil-lamps with sooty mantles, their brass fittings gleaming in the hazy orange light.

Esteban led her down the passageway and turned right into an octagonal room with smooth stone walls, lined with cases of books which reached from the stone-flagged floor to the beamed ceiling. To one side were a desk and bosun's chair, to the other a library table strewn with old books. The fireplace was a fantastical creation of carved wood, the faces of demons peering out from between ornately carved fronds of fern and mistletoe. Despite the sultry warmth of the night a fire burned in the hearth, the dancing flames casting shadows on the walls and ceiling, throwing the carvings into ghoulish relief so that, for a few seconds, Venetia almost believed they were alive.

'I . . . had to come,' Venetia blurted out, hardly knowing where to begin.

Esteban was standing beside the desk, his face half in light, half in shade. He seemed more mysterious and enigmatic than ever.

'Evidently,' he said quietly. 'Will you take a glass of wine, Venetia?'

With perfect composure, he took two glasses from a wall-cabinet and filled them from a bottle on the windowsill. Beyond the windows, dusk was closing in over the bay, the distant sea reduced to a dark line on the horizon, dotted with sparks of white light as the full moon rose over Valazur.

He handed Venetia a glass. The wine was blood-red, thick and rich, its bouquet potent and heady. Esteban's eyes never left her face as she drank. She could feel the heat of his gaze penetrating her very soul as the heat of the wine trickled slowly and sensually down her throat, burning and seducing.

Esteban leaned back against the desk, casual and confident in black trousers and a white, loose-cut shirt which seemed to caress the clean lines of his spare yet muscular body. Draining his glass, he refilled it from the bottle. He seemed perfectly at ease whilst Venetia felt overwhelmed and afraid, sexually potent and profoundly vulnerable, all at once.

'If you have something to say to me, *petite anglaise*, you had better say it,' remarked Esteban coolly. Venetia couldn't help noticing that the top two buttons of his shirt were undone, revealing little curls of dark hair lying against the light olive skin of his chest. Oh, how she longed to kiss them . . .

'I read Peterson's diary, and his notes,' she told him, almost as afraid of her own sexuality as she was of the situation in which she now found herself.

'And?'

And he talks about some weird sex-cult. He says Levigny is involved in it, and Defarge . . . and God knows how many others, maybe half of Valazur.'

'I see.' Esteban held his glass up to the light, turning it slowly round so that the candlelight caught the many facets and turned the ruby-red wine to liquid fire. 'And you decided to come to me to ask me what you should do?'

'I suppose so . . . yes.'

'That makes no sense at all, my dear Venetia. How do you know that I too am not a member of this so-called cult?'

'I don't,' replied Venetia.

'Then you are either very brave or very foolhardly. Which is it, Venetia?'

She saw his eyes glitter as he smiled. Was he mocking her? Or could he really see into her soul, as she feared he could? Could he really feel, and touch, and taste and smell the desire pouring out from her, soaking into the gusset of her white lace panties?

'I came here to get answers, Esteban,' she told him, her voice suddenly firm and decisive.

'I told you at the casino. I have none to give you.'

'I want to know the truth, Esteban!'

His lips curved into a smile. 'Then you must find it out for yourself.'

'For fuck's sake, Esteban. I demand to know the truth!' Venetia's temper snapped, and in a sudden fury she flung the wine-glass at the wall. It struck the stonework behind Esteban's head and exploded in a shower of diamond-bright fragments, leaving a wet mass of sacrificial red, dripping down the wall on to the white goatskin rug.

For a moment, she stood frozen in horrified contemplation of what she had just done. How would Esteban react? Would he throw her out of his house? He had every right to. Would he do to her what Peterson had seen Levigny doing to some poor, nameless girl . . .?

Esteban drained his second glass of wine, regarded the glass for a moment then, with sudden laughter, threw it into the fireplace. It flared up momentarily, cracking and sizzling as the last few drops of red wine evaporated.

'You have more spirit than I gave you credit for,' he commented, walking across the room to where Venetia was standing. She could feel electricity crackling and arcing between them, even before his fingers touched her hand, lifting it to his lips, kissing it. 'My adorable English vixen . . .'

'Esteban, please – there are so many questions I have to ask you. Please!'

'All questions can wait.' His lips parted and his tongue licked slowly and sensually over Venetia's fingers, taking her index finger right into his mouth and sucking it before allowing it to escape, glistening with saliva. 'Hunger cannot.'

Venetia was trembling. Her whole body was shaking, out of control, the little composure she had had left evaporating like the wine Esteban had thrown on to the fire. What was happening to her? She tried to move but she couldn't. Why? Because she didn't want to. Something deep and dark and undeniable in her own soul demanded that she must stay, that she must answer the call of the searing, gnawing hunger in her belly.

'I don't know what you mean,' she gasped. 'Please . . . you must let me go.'

'You are wet for me,' whispered Esteban, drawing her towards him and kissing her throat. His lips felt cool, his breath like a summer breeze on her bare skin. 'Do not deny it, Venetia, I can smell your desire.'

She could not speak. Desire had closed up her throat, made her mouth dry and parched. It was as though all the wetness in her entire body had concentrated itself in the sodden triangle of lace between her thighs. Fragrant juices were flooding out of her, welling up, trickling, dripping down her bare, tanned thighs.

'Ah. Ah, oh . . .' she moaned, wordless, lost in the red mist of her desire, so long frustrated, so long suppressed.

'Beauty should never be ashamed,' Esteban told her, his fingers working feverishly at the zipper which ran down the back of her short, tight summer dress. 'Beauty should go naked.'

The zipper yielded with a long sighing whisper, and Venetia felt Esteban's fingers stroking down the long, smooth curve of her back, awakening new and delicious levels of sensation, so long hidden, so long unsuspected.

Suddenly Esteban seemed so different – no longer the cold, emotionless man who had sent her away. His coldness had turned to the fire of hunger, his almost obsessive detachment to a raging passion. He kissed her, full on the lips now, his lips crushing hers again and again, the wetness of their mouths dripping and mingling, their tongues jousting, signalling their shared hunger.

He stripped her dress from her shoulders, down over the tingling crests of her nipples, the tautness of her belly and the rounded swell of hip and thigh. It fell to the ground and she stood before him in her bra, panties and shoes.

She felt his hardness pressing against her belly as he took her into his arms, the long, thick rod of his manhood pushing and pressing against the inner surface of his trousers, pleading for the caress of liberation. A caress she so dearly wished to bestow.

Hunger overtook her, and she began kissing him – greedily, passionately, her teeth nipping his flesh as she bared it, unfastening the first few buttons of his shirt then growing impatient and ripping it from his back, baring his torso.

He was tall and slimly built, but with the discreet hint of muscle beneath tanned, taut flesh. An old, deep scar ran from one shoulder, diagonally down to below his waist. Venetia traced it with her fingertips.

'Esteban. How . . .?'

'Questions can wait,' he silenced her, his mouth covering hers, his tongue penetrating her with a lover's insistence. 'But I cannot wait for you, my English one. Already I have waited too long.'

His fingers reached into the lacy cups of her underwired bra, seizing hold of her breasts and pulling them out, so that they lay like ripe melons on the wire cradle beneath them. A network of fine bluish veins stood out against the pale golden flesh, and the nipples were turgid stalks of the deepest pink. His fingers rubbed and pinched them, and Venetia began to moan and writhe at his cruelly pleasurable caresses.

'Oh . . . I can't bear it. Oh Esteban . . .'

He whispered to her as he made love to her with his fingers and tongue.

'Did you see me in your dreams, Venetia? Did you? I have dreamed of you. We were in a golden cage, hanging over a deep, dark sea . . .'

Lost in the world of her desire, Venetia did not even wonder how Esteban could possibly know about her dream – a dream which she had not spoken about to anyone. All she cared about was the desperate excitement of the moment, the feeling of flesh on flesh, the touch of Esteban's fingers and lips on her nipples, the hardness of his thigh between her legs, gently and salaciously rubbing her to the brink of madness as he pushed her back until she was half-standing, half-lying across the old library table.

Books and papers scattered in all directions as she sank down on to the table. Her fingers fumbled with Esteban's belt. At last the buckle yielded, then the row of ivory buttons leading from his waist-band down his flies. And as her hand slipped inside, she discovered a truth which sent joy singing through every nerve and fibre in her body.

Naked. He was naked underneath; his man-hood a stiff, smooth spear of flesh, his testes round, ripe fruits covered in downy-soft, black curls. And as his large, erect penis sprang into her hand, her fingers discovered a stranger, still more arousing truth.

For Esteban was pierced. A ring of iridescent black haematite passed through his glans, the smooth stone carved into the shape of a serpent with its tail in its mouth. As the light caught it it glimmered and shone like polished metal, and drops of lubricating fluid welled up from Esteban's cock-tip and began dripping over the ring, smearing over Venetia's fingers.

As she touched him, Esteban let out a long, low groan of need.

'Softly, Venetia. Softly . . . you will make me come and I have only just begun.'

'Touch me,' pleaded Venetia, close to tears. 'Don't leave me like this, touch me. Take me . . .'

'We have both waited too long,' murmured Esteban, reaching out for a knife which lay amid the scattered papers. It was razor-sharp, a jewel-handled dagger with a silver hilt. Venetia's eyes widened in alarm and she let out a cry as the blade touched her thigh and slid suddenly upwards, slitting through the side of her lace panties.

Left and right; the two narrow strips of stretchy lace yielded easily to the blade, and Esteban slid the useless scrap of material from between Venetia's thighs. He pressed it to his face, breathing in the potent fragrance of her need. Venetia felt his cock stiffen in her hands, knew that if she were only to stroke it, give it the gentlest of caresses, it would spit its venom onto the burning heart of her sex.

'You have the body of an angel and the scent of a harlot,' whispered Esteban. 'Were you sent to this earth to torment me for all eternity?'

His hands stroked up the inner surface of her thighs, and she quivered at his touch, her hips swaying and grinding on the table, her sex gaping wide and pleading for one kiss, one caress to liberate it from its torment.

'Please, Esteban, yes. Yes . . .'

A single sword-thrust was all it took to enter her, Esteban's penis scything into the soft flesh, its wetness welcoming him in. Venetia screamed out in sudden pleasure, her back arching off the table as he clutched at her buttocks, forcing himself so deeply into her that she could feel his testicles pushing and rubbing at the entrance to her vagina.

Venetia's fingers clawed at Esteban's back, so convulsively that her nails left red tracks, swelling into weals on the tanned golden skin. They were no longer two separate individuals, but one passionate creation, a unity of matchless passion.

Venetia lost all track of time and space. She scarcely even remembered who she was, only that with each thrust of Esteban's hips he was bringing her a little nearer to the merciful release of ecstasy. She had never experienced love-making like this before. It was neither sophisticated nor skilful, yet the sheer raw passion of their fucking sent sparks of electricity flying into the night air. Esteban's cock-ring pressed hard against the neck of Venetia's womb, the smooth stone distending the delicate, spongy walls of her vagina and seeking out, with unerring precision, the g-spot which could turn orgasm into ecstasy.

Their bodies dripped sweat; their lips mouthed wordless songs of pleasure; and as dusk turned to the velvet black of night, so their hunger turned to the first, warm glow of fulfilment.

Wave upon wave; crashing down on the shore of their need. White, foaming waves of ecstasy, as Esteban's cock spurted semen and Venetia's sex-muscles tensed, as though she never wanted to let him go.

Later, when pleasure had ebbed away and hunger had returned, they would walk up the winding stone staircase to Esteban's bedroom. And there, in the dark silence of the night, it would begin again.

Chapter Six

VENETIA SCARCELY KNEW where dream met reality.

That night, with Esteban, she experienced passion she had only ever known in dreams; and yet she could feel his caresses, taste and smell and touch his passion as they coupled again and again.

Time seemed to have lost its meaning. Seconds melted into hours through the long, velvet night, and the only measure of the passing hours was the ebb and flow of the lovers' hunger.

How had it begun? What spark had lit the flame of their passion, and made it burn, furnace-bright, through the sweet, dark hours? What strange metamorphosis had transformed Esteban from cool, distant stranger to the intensely passionate lover beside her? Venetia asked no questions, lost in the obsession of her desire, a desire so clearly shared by Esteban.

She had never known such pleasure, never dreamed such thrills of ecstasy. An almost magical energy sparked between them, electric shocks of excitement filling her with an erotic tension so delicious she wanted it to last for ever and ever and never end.

'I have waited ... waited so long ...' he whispered to her as she lay on her belly on the crisp white sheets, and he slid his stiff rod into the welcoming haven between her moist thighs.

And it seemed to Venetia that she had been waiting all her life for a man like Esteban to awaken the latent sensuality within her. Ramon had been a diverting distraction from the boredom of her work; Bastien an exciting dalliance with sophisticated sensuality. But what she was sharing with Esteban was raw, passionate, the hunger of two beasts rutting in a forest, at once brutal and tender.

When at last she fell asleep, it was to dream of Esteban.

She awoke alone, the sheets damp and cold, the bedroom no longer suffused with the pale glamour of moonlight but flooded by a fierce, unforgiving sunshine which blazed in through the half-open curtains.

'Esteban?'

She rolled over, feeling for him, but his head was not on the pillow beside her. Nor were his clothes on the floor where he had thrown them in his hunger to bed her. She was quite, quite alone.

Puzzled, she slid out of bed and padded into the bathroom which opened off the bedroom. A warm, fresh scent filled the room and she breathed it in. Lilacs. Fresh, spring lilacs. She glanced down and saw that the Victorian enamelled bath was two-thirds full of foaming, scented water. She tested it with her finger. It was exactly the right temperature.

Perhaps Esteban had run the bath for himself, and would be back in a moment. She waited, but no one came. Walking back to the bedroom door, she looked outside, and called his name, but the empty corridor echoed it back in an eerie whisper.

'Esteban, Esteban, Esteban . . .'

It was almost as if she were alone in the house. Surely he couldn't have gone off and left her – not after the night of passion they had just spent together. Or hadn't it meant anything to him? Had Esteban simply taken advantage of her desire for him? But no, that couldn't be right. She'd felt the desire throbbing inside him, she even bore the marks on her breasts and belly, where his nails had clawed at her flesh in the frenzy of his passion.

Venetia walked back into the bathroom, intending to see what sort of a mess she looked this morning, but to her surprise there was no mirror. What sort of a place was this? You'd have thought a man like Esteban would be so vain that he couldn't stop admiring himself in the mirror – or maybe he was so confident of his beauty that he didn't need to look.

Well, if Esteban wasn't coming back, she might as well enjoy his bathwater before it got cold. Dipping her toe into the water, she found it warm and welcoming as a tropical lagoon, the lilac-scent wafting around her, engulfing her with its innocently sensual perfume.

She lay back in the bath, sliding down under the thick raft of bubbles which lay in peaks across the surface of the water. This was sheer, unadulterated luxury. The only thing that bothered her was Esteban. Where the hell could he have got to?

After her bath, she put on a robe and went back into the bedroom to get dressed. To her astonishment she found a silver tray on the bedside table. It held a glass of wine, a bowl of fruit and a white envelope, across which had been scrawled a single word in sepia-coloured ink.

Venetia.

That was odd. How could anyone have got into the room to put the tray there while she was in the bath? Surely she would have heard someone coming into the bedroom? Hurriedly she tore open the envelope, her heart thumping in her chest.

The words she read tightened a cold hand about her heart.

Venetia, you must leave now. Last night was a weakness on my part, it will not happen again. I feel nothing for you, you must understand that. Nothing at all. This must not be.

'No!' A gasp of pain escaped from Venetia's lips.

It wasn't true, it couldn't be. The memory of Esteban's kisses, his caresses, the sensual artistry of his love-making, remained with her as vividly as if they had only just parted. If she closed her eyes she could see him, feel his arms about her waist, his long, pierced cock pushing into her warm, wet haven.

And no perfumed bath could not wash away the clinging scent of their shared passion, that unique fragrance of mingled sex-juices, spicy and strong. She had *felt* his passion, lived it. What he said could not be true. But why . . .? Whatever did he mean when he said 'this must not be'?

She read on.

You must also leave Valazur. There is great danger for you here. I cannot be responsible for the consequences if you choose to ignore my warning.

Go now. Never return. Forget you ever met me, petite anglaise.

Esteban.

She sank down on to the side of the bed, momentarily too stunned to think clearly. This scribbled note . . . what did it mean? That Esteban had been using her all along, just using her to satisfy his desires, and that he was now casting her off?

The first pain of sorrow was replaced by the slow burn of anger. How could he do this to her? How could he think that he could just talk her into his bed and then tell her to get out of his house?

Well, she wasn't going to waste any more time here, that was for sure. She wasn't going to hang around and wait to be thrown out like yesterday's papers. Slowly and deliberately, Venetia tore the letter into tiny fragments and, leaning out of the open window, held out her hand and watched the breeze snatch them away, scattering them like whirling snowflakes.

Whatever Esteban might think, he wasn't going to have everything his own way. If Esteban wanted her out of his life, he would first have to prove that he had nothing to do with Cassie's disappearance.

And when he had done that, he would have to prove to Venetia that the passion they had shared was a lie.

Venetia walked through the house, through a maze of corridors, dimly-lit even in the brightness of a summer's morning. The windows were tiny, she thought to herself as she glanced about her. Great looming passageways with rough stone walls, or lined with dark wooden panelling, lent the old house a gloomy, almost organic feel. It was like walking through the entrails of some great beast, feeling its heart beating beneath her feet.

And yet there was a certain Gothic beauty to the place. Beautiful artifacts, objects of great antiquity and rare loveliness, peeped out at her from half-hidden corners. The furniture was a jumble from many ages, Louis XV *fauteuils* alongside a carved Breton chest and a medieval painted chair. Carvings and statuettes lined the hallway, faces and hands stretched out towards her, as though beseeching her to stay.

The house was deserted, silent as the grave. Not even the ticking of a clock disturbed the great and solemn stillness. Only the sound of her feet tapping on the flagstones awoke the slumbering echoes.

Anger still burned within her as she released the latch on the front door and turned to survey what she was leaving behind her.

'Good riddance,' she spat, under her breath; but inside she was empty and afraid, and all she longed for was Esteban's touch, the kisses he was so cruelly denying her.

She walked out into the sunshine, slamming the door behind her. The heavy wooden door closed with a shuddering crash which seemed to reverberate through the entire house. The battered old Citroën was still parked outside, looking even shabbier in the morning light. If she was sticking around Valazur she would have to see if she could afford to rent a better runabout. And she *was* sticking around, no matter what that bastard Esteban might say.

The car started first time, and she drove slowly down the driveway, the gates swinging open automatically as she approached, then gliding silently shut behind her, as though signalling that this was the end of something which had scarcely begun. Well, Esteban might be able to dismiss their passion in a few words, but Venetia could not. Her hunger burned more brightly than ever, a flame which, once kindled, would not easily be extinguished.

Driving out on to the coast road, she wound down the windows and tried to relax. Put him out of her mind, that was the thing to do. She turned on the radio-cassette player and the latest Euro-pop blared out, trashy and loud, pushing the bad thoughts out of her mind.

She'd go back to the villa, pick up her stuff, move out. That was the best thing to do, the *only* thing to do. With what she knew about Léonore and Levigny, and the stuff Peterson had written in his diary, she wasn't at all sure she wanted to hang around the Villa Le Rocq much longer. It was always remotely possible that Léonore had something to do with Cassie's disappearance, though it was probably something and nothing. Yes, she couldn't even be sure that what Peterson had said was true . . .

But she really must sort things out, get away from the Villa. Put some distance between herself and Bastien. Getting involved with Bastien had been a big mistake, she knew that now. Now she didn't know who she could trust. Certainly not Esteban.

As she steered round a sharp bend, the car engine coughed, spluttered and died.

'Damn!'

Venetia tried to restart the engine but all it managed was a bronchitic wheeze. It couldn't be the petrol tank – the car had been filled up only the night before.

She got out of the car and slammed the door, aiming a poorly-judged kick at the front offside wheel. On the car stereo some Belgian band was still chirruping along to the latest techno hit.

'Forty thousand bloody damns!'

The sound of an engine on the road behind her made her turn round. A gleaming silver Mercedes was gliding round the corner towards her, the driver's face obscured by the sunlight flaring in a starburst from the windscreen. It slowed down and parked just behind her, and the driver got out, smoothing the creases out of his designer trousers.

'Ta voiture est en panne, ma chère?'

'Bastien!' Venetia felt hot and cold. 'But I thought you weren't supposed to be coming back to Valazur until tomorrow.'

Bastien shrugged, thrusting his hands casually into his pockets and strolling towards her. He was good-looking, sure he was. Wavy golden-brown hair, clean-cut features, athletic body. It was easy to see how she could have fallen instantly in lust with him. But that was all over now – wasn't it?

'I decided to come home a little early . . . to see you, *chérie*. I thought perhaps we could spent the rest of the day together.'

'Oh. I . . .' How was she going to tell him? 'I was thinking of moving out,' she stuttered.

Bastien's eyebrows arched in surprise.

'Moving out of the Villa Le Rocq? But what on earth for, *chérie*? You do not find our hospitality pleasing?' He reached out and touched Venetia's arm. 'You do not find me pleasing, perhaps?'

'It's just . . . yes, of course I like you, Bastien. It's just that I think perhaps we should just be friends.'

Bastien's face broke into a handsome grin. 'Friends? Why, of course, *chère* Venetia.' He gave her a kiss on the cheek, which turned into a kiss on her throat, her neck, her shoulder.

'Please, Bastien . . .'

'But even friends can be passionate, Venetia.' He glanced up the hill, towards Esteban's villa.

'You have been visiting friends perhaps, Venetia?'

'Sort of.'

Bastien drew her towards him and although she wanted to pull away, the seductive lure of his warmth was too much to bear. She found herself clinging to him, desperate for the comfort of his embraces after Esteban's sudden rejection.

'You should keep away from men like him, Venetia,' whispered Bastien, caressing her hair. 'Esteban is worthless.' He spat on the ground, emphasising his contempt. 'He will bring you nothing but pain.'

'I . . . I know.'

Venetia's breath escaped in a shuddering sob of distress, and suddenly she was in Bastien's arms and he was kissing her tears away, his hands smoothing and kneading her backside, pressing her to him, possessing her once again with his kisses.

'Come home with me, Venetia. I know how to give you pleasure, no one knows better than I.'

She allowed herself to be led to Bastien's car and he held the passenger door open for her.

'Leave the Citroën here, *chérie*. I will arrange for it to be removed. A beautiful woman like you deserves to travel in style. If you will only permit me, I shall take the greatest care of you, Venetia Fellowes.'

*

The Villa Le Rocq seemed surprisingly welcoming as the Mercedes approached and glided into the long, sweeping driveway. Noonday sunshine made the white walls gleam, and the terracotta roof-tiles glowed with warmth.

Bastien was as good as his word, solicitous to a fault. He opened the door for her and took her hand, drawing her out. She felt childlike and vulnerable beside him, the coldness within her heart reaching out to his warmth and hugging it to her, wanting to believe that this man, at least, cared for her and desired her for his own.

'Léonore is away at some art exhibition in Cannes,' Bastien told her as they walked through into the hallway. 'And the servants will not be back until this evening. Come into the kitchen. Oh, *chérie*, you're so cold. What you need is a drink.'

'It's rather early . . .' Venetia began, but Bastien closed her mouth with a kiss.

'It is never too early for the finest champagne,' he reproved her, and then he laughed – so infectiously that despite her misgivings, Venetia found herself joining in.

Bastien reached into the refrigerator and took out a bottle of his favourite Veuve Clicquot, took two champagne flutes from a cupboard and set them down on the table. Venetia drew up a chair and watched him deftly unscrewing the wire cage, then easing out the cork with his thumbs.

'*Attention, chérie . . . ça vient!*' The cork shot out of the bottle with a loud pop and hit the wall behind Venetia's head. A cascade of white foaming champagne streamed out of the bottle and large, foamy droplets fell on to Venetia's dress, making the fabric transparent and clingy.

Bastien filled a glass and handed it to Venetia.

'Oh, I don't know, Bastien . . . I shouldn't really.'

'*Chérie*, it will do you good.'

'Perhaps. But I don't think . . .'

She found herself looking into Bastien's eyes. Their soft green-grey made her heart race, despite her determination to resist his gently seductive persuasion.

'*Chérie* . . . for me? Just one glass?'

'Well . . . I don't suppose one glass will do any harm.'

She raised the glass to her lips.

'*Santé*,' said Bastien. And she drank, not noticing that Bastien was taking only the tiniest of sips from his glass.

The champagne tasted wonderful – much better than she had remembered. Bastien was right – champagne really did revive you, gave you a sense of luxury. It tasted like liquid sunshine.

'I feel like a princess,' she giggled, as the icy-cold liquid trickled down her throat and awakened a warm, slow, burning in the pit of her stomach.

'And so you are,' smiled Bastien, setting his own glass down on the table. 'You are as beautiful as a queen, Venetia – *non*! A goddess, at the very least.'

She tried to put her hand over her glass but suddenly she felt rather uncoordinated and woozy. Not unpleasantly so, in fact the feeling was intensely pleasurable; a warm giddiness which made her whole body relax and banish whatever was left of its foolish inhibitions.

Bastien gently lifted her hand from the glass and topped it up.

'*Encore un tout petit peu?*' he whispered, and he lifted her hand to her lips. He had no need to persuade her, for she was already parting her lips to drink, taking the crystal-clear wine into her mouth, feeling it fizz on her tongue and then slide, smooth as ice, down her throat.

What on earth was happening to her? She passed her hand over her eyes, half-heartedly trying to bring her sight back into focus. She felt ridiculously giggly and it was wonderful – like being a silly kid again, freed from all the constraints of sensible womanhood.

'Bastien!' she exclaimed, trying to focus on him. 'I can see . . . I can see two of you!'

It seemed the funniest thing in the world, and she heard herself laugh. It was like hearing herself laugh at the other end of a very long, very narrow corridor, but that didn't worry her. Nothing at all could worry her, not feeling like this.

'Don't worry, sweet Venetia.' Bastien reached behind her and started undoing her dress, pushing down the tag so that, millimetre by millimetre, her bare back appeared. 'Don't worry, I'll look after you. You see, *chérie*, I know exactly what you want.'

'Bastien, you bad boy – you shouldn't. Really, you shouldn't!'

Venetia could hear herself protesting, but her body was singing a welcome to Bastien's greedy fingers. She wondered, very vaguely, somewhere at the back of her mind, exactly why she should feel like this, all of a sudden; but it didn't seem important, not really. Nothing seemed important except the chance to feel Bastien undressing her, showing her the way to find true pleasure.

That's right. Surely it was right. It wasn't Esteban she wanted, not really. It was Bastien. It must be Bastien. Didn't he keep telling her so?

Bastien's eyes gleamed in triumph. It had taken time, patience, planning; but at last he had the little English girl exactly where he wanted her – utterly, completely in his power. Now he was going to enjoy himself, showing Venetia exactly what it was that her body and soul truly craved.

Chapter Seven

'WELCOME, VENETIA. WE are so glad that you could join us.'

Venetia awoke to the sound of eerie, mocking laughter, echoing around and around her head. She struggled to open her eyes but they felt heavy as lead. And what was that low, dull ache throbbing in her neck and shoulders? What was wrong with her arms . . .? They were stretched up above her head, something hard and cold binding them together, and she was hanging from them, her feet only just touching the ground.

'Open your eyes, Venetia. We want you to see us. We want our new slave to see her temple.'

She thought she half-recognised the voice, but she couldn't quite place it. Something touched her skin . . . a hand, stroking down the curve of her bare backside. It made her shiver with revulsion.

'Bastien . . .? No, please . . .'

Her eyes flickered open, and she found herself looking not at Bastien, but straight into the eyes of Jean-Marc Levigny.

His hands moved to her breasts, clutching great handfuls of the soft flesh, squeezing so hard that Venetia squirmed and yelped with discomfort. But there was no escaping from Levigny's cruel caress. Her wrists were held fast in heavy iron manacles, attached to a long chain which was threaded through an iron ring set into the ceiling.

'*Monsieur!*' she gasped. 'Please . . . what are you doing to me? Let me go . . .'

Levigny laughed; a dark and menacing laugh which filled her with terror.

'Let you go, Venetia? Now, why would we want to let you go when we have spent so much time and trouble to bring you here?'

'Why . . .? Why are you doing this to me?'

She twisted and turned in her chains, her eyes darting wildly about her, looking for someone, something that might give her hope of escape. But what she saw filled her only with despair.

There were four other people in the chamber: Bastien Le Rocq, Inspector Defarge, Gérard and Bastien's cousin Léonore. They were standing in a circle around Venetia, dressed in long capes of scarlet and black velvet which fell open at the front to reveal their nakedness beneath.

The chamber in which they stood was airless, windowless, chill and damp. The floor was of smooth white marble, and the same stone had been used to create round pillars and colonnades in a classical style. It was lit by lanterns which hung from the vaulted ceiling, casting a wash of pale gold over everything.

To one side stood a large block of the same white marble, smooth on the top, like some kind of altar table, but with elaborate carvings on the sides. Carvings of men and women indulging in an orgy of frenzied coupling . . . Copper braziers burned on either side, wisps of sweetly scented smoke curling into the air from smouldering piles of aromatic woods and herbs.

'Please . . . Léonore . . . do something. Tell them to let me go,' she begged, appealing to Bastien's cousin. Surely another woman would not stand by and watch this happening to her.

'But if we let you go, we would not have you for our ritual,' smiled Léonore, parting the folds of her cape and running her hands lasciviously over her own breasts. 'And you will make such an adorable temple slave, Venetia.'

'Bastien! For pity's sake . . .!' Anger welled up in Venetia's throat and she screamed her rage at him, kicking out her legs, trying to do something, anything to hurt these people who had done this

144

to her. Oh why hadn't she been more careful? Why had she allowed Bastien Le Rocq to seduce her in the first place? Why hadn't she listened to Esteban and got the hell out of Valazur?

Now, it seemed that she had walked straight into hell itself.

'Pity, *chérie*? There is no pity here, only pleasure.' Bastien walked forward, insolently handsome, his golden-brown hair glossy in the pale light from the gently swaying lanterns.

'But why . . .?' pleaded Venetia. 'Tell me why. It was you, wasn't it? What have you done with my sister?'

'You ask too many questions, Mademoiselle Fellowes,' remarked Inspector Defarge, a massive man of forty-five, heavily-built and with a huge cock hanging semi-erect between his muscular thighs. Venetia shuddered at his approach, terrified by the thought of what a man like that might do to a woman, helpless and in chains, utterly at the mercy of his voracious desire.

'You should never have come to Valazur,' observed Gérard. 'We tried to tell you, but you would not listen. *Chère Venetia*, what a little fool you have been.'

'You see,' explained Bastien, reaching out and taking hold of Venetia's right nipple between his finger and thumb, 'once you discovered Peterson's diary there could be no possible escape for you. Had Peterson lived longer, he too would have . . . served our needs.'

'You killed Peterson?'

'No. Peterson's murder was nothing to do with the Elect. But it came at a most convenient moment, and for that we are grateful. Whoever killed Evan Peterson saved us the trouble of doing it.'

'Beasts!' screeched Venetia, her voice high and shrill.

'Not beasts, Venetia,' replied Levigny. 'We prefer to think of ourselves as connoisseurs – sexual gourmets, if you like. And our sensual experiments also serve to empower our rituals.'

'Rituals? I . . .'

'This place.' Levigny indicated the chamber with a broad sweep of his hand. 'This is the Temple of the Elect, a religious sect which has been in existence since the first century AD, when the Romans still ruled in Valazur, in fact in all of what they called Provincia Romana. Our forefathers created this temple, hewn from caves beneath what is now the church of St Agnès, and through the centuries our ancient families have kept the old ways alive.'

'There is power in sex,' said Defarge. 'Did you know that, my pretty one? Great power.' He was standing in plain sight of her, cradling his swelling dick in his two hands, presenting its obscene shaft to her as though it were a gift.

Defarge leered at Venetia. 'Do you remember

the first day you came to see me at the *Commissariat de Police*?' he demanded. 'I remember it well. You were sitting on one side of my desk, wearing that tight white T-shirt and those tiny cotton shorts. And you were asking me so many questions, always questions, Venetia. And now your questions have led you back to me, to us, for our pleasure.'

He laughed, well pleased with the look of intense fear and disgust on Venetia's face. She wanted to look away, to deny him the satisfaction of her terror, but she couldn't tear her eyes away from the massive, threatening presence of his immensely swollen dick.

'Patience, *ma soeur*,' smiled Levigny with consummate irony. 'In time you will feel the power of Brother Defarge's desire. But first there are other pleasures for you to undergo.'

Bastien now ran his hand up between Venetia's thighs, and she kicked out, writhing furiously in an attempt to escape from his unwelcome caresses.

'Perhaps we should chain her more securely,' volunteered Defarge. 'We could secure her ankles so that she cannot resist. Or drug her again.' He laughed. 'The drugged champagne had a most satisfactory effect.'

'No.' Levigny shook his head emphatically. 'There will be much greater pleasure in breaking her spirit if there are no artificial restraints or

147

sedatives.' A slow smile crept over his handsome yet sublimely evil features. 'She will make a passable slave. And when we have done with her, and have sated ourselves on her ripe body, an even better blood sacrifice.'

Laughter rang around the temple, and even in the haze of Levigny's words, Venetia's blood turned to ice. A blood-sacrifice! They could not, surely they could not . . .

'Feel the power, Brothers,' said Levigny. 'Feel the sensual power of this new slave. She is worthy of the ritual. Bring forth the other slave.'

The other slave . . .? Up till now, Venetia had believed herself alone, so very alone in this place. Was there some other poor girl here too, sharing the torment, waiting for the moment of release . . .?

Of sacrifice?

She raised her head to see Léonore leading in a girl, naked and covered in painted magical symbols. Her ankles were hobbled with a short chain, and her wrists were shackled behind her back. Long blonde hair fell in tangled, matted waves down her back.

The girl looked up and her eyes met Venetia's; but there was no sign of recognition. She was sunk too deep in her drugged haze to feel or see anything. But Venetia recognised her. She recognised her only too well.

'Cassie,' she whispered. And for a few seconds,

time seemed to stop in its tracks.

'Cassie ... oh Cassie, it's me, don't you know me? Cassie, please look at me!' Venetia turned blazing eyes on Jean-Marc Levigny. 'What have you done to her? What have you done to my sister?'

Levigny threw back his head and laughed.

'*Ma chère petite*. What spirit you have. A spirit which I shall have great pleasure in breaking.' He walked across to where Léonore and Cassie were standing. 'Unlock the manacles and ankle chains. I wish to make *une petite exposition* ... I shall demonstrate to you, Mademoiselle Venetia, how completely your slut of a sister has accepted the disciplines which we have taught her during her ... stay with us.'

Venetia renewed her struggles, knowing it was hopeless, but knowing also that she must do something or go mad. Guilt swamped her. She was the older twin, the responsible one – or at least, she'd always felt responsible for Cassie. Cassie who had always got herself into scrapes as a child and who had now got them both into the biggest, deepest trouble of their entire lives.

She squashed up her fingers and tried to pull her hand through the manacle, but it was too tight and her wrist had swelled a little, making the task yet more impossible.

'I would advise you not to struggle,' said

Bastien, cool, calm and almost expressionless, the only signs of his immense satisfaction the half-smile twitching the corners of his mouth, and the rearing head of his hardening dick. 'We shall only be obliged to punish you.'

Venetia was certain the others must be able to hear her heart thumping in her chest, her blood pounding through her veins. Her chest heaved, her quivering breasts wet with sweat. She glared at her captors, her eyes flashing fire; and with all the remaining strength within her, she lied.

'I am not afraid of you. Any of you.'

'That is a pity, Venetia,' observed Defarge, almost sorrowfully. 'Because really, *ma chère*, I think that you should be very afraid.'

Léonore unlocked the iron cuffs around Cassie's hands and feet, and for a moment Venetia had a wild hope that perhaps her dazed state was feigned; that once she was free, Cassie would make an attempt at escape. But it was not to be. Cassie stood, docile and dull-eyed, making no move to resist anything which was done to her.

'Are you happy, Cassandra?' Levigny's voice was soft, caressing.

Cassie turned her face a little towards him, but she seemed to be looking right through him to something very far away.

'I . . . I am happy.' Her voice was a flat monotone, and anger clutched and squeezed at

150

Venetia's heart, sending a dull pain through her, making her long for vengeance.

'What is it that you most want to do, Cassandra?'

There was a moment's hesitation, as though Cassie were trying to remember something that she had been taught by rote, and then she replied, 'To obey.'

Levigny wheeled round to look at Venetia, smiling smugly.

'You see, *chère* Venetia, your sister wants nothing more than to obey our every desire. You too will learn the joys of obedience before we have finished with your pretty body.

'Tonight we shall use you both in a ritual of conjuration, a rite in which we shall call up the ancient spirits of those who have gone before us. Spirits which will renew the great power which the ancient ways have already given us. And you, *ma chère anglaise*, will assist us in our conjuration.'

Venetia spat at Levigny, a glistening blob of spittle landing a few inches in front of his feet.

'Go to hell!'

'Such a temper deserves to be tamed, Venetia.'

'I shall do nothing – nothing to help you, you understand?'

'My dear Venetia, you will do absolutely everything we demand of you. If you do not, *both* you and Cassie will die – tonight.'

Venetia aroused him even more than Cassie

did. For Cassie's spirit was broken, whereas Venetia was still a spitting fury, a man-eating tigress who must be tamed and enslaved to his will.

She and her sister together would make an admirable sacrifice. Identical twins! The Elect had dreamed of such good fortune for years. With both Cassie and Venetia as their obedient 'priestesses', they would be able to perform a ritual of such magical potency that the Elect would achieve wealth and dominion not just in Valazur but in all the wealthy towns along the French Riviera. With such occult power they would not, could not fail.

'The omens are favourable.' he announced. 'We may commence the ceremony of conjuration. Chain Cassandra to the altar.'

Venetia, freed now from the manacles which had held her prisoner, darted forward, trying to get to her sister, but Defarge prevented her, his bear's-paw hands seizing her roughly by the shoulders and holding her back.

'Cease your struggling, slave. If you do not, we have ways of making you.'

Venetia detected a note of real hunger in his voice. Compared to Cassie she might be something of a sexual innocent, but she was aware enough to know that of all the cult members, it was Defarge that she should fear most. Defarge saw her as more than an object of ritual significance, more than a catalyst for some magical hocus-pocus. He saw her as his sexual plaything, wanted her for his possession. Wanted to use, abuse and destroy her with his desire.

Shackles were placed around Cassie's wrists and ankles and she was chained, face-up, on the altar.

'Please . . . what are you doing to her? Let her go. Whatever you are going to do, please, choose me instead,' pleaded Venetia, but Defarge only laughed.

'Such impatience, *ma jolie anglaise*. Such an impetuous slut you are. But have no fear, you too shall share in the power of our ritual.'

Soft music was playing, somewhere in the background. It was impossible to tell where it was coming from. It was low, sensual, the sinuous sounds of swooping flutes and oboes, filling her head with images of sex. Brother Gérard held a censer, which he swung from a long golden chain, filling the temple with heady clouds of white incense.

Venetia felt dizzy and disorientated. Defarge was leading her by the hand through the white mist of incense, towards the altar where Cassie lay. There must have been some powerful aphrodisiac in the incense, for she felt both detached and aroused.

The music was getting louder, and behind her her captors were chanting some weird incantation.

She didn't understand it. It sounded a little like Latin, mixed with fragments of old French. Now she was standing beside the altar, looking down at Cassie. Their eyes met, and for the first time she saw the clouds melting away, the first glimmer of recognition in those blue eyes, a reflection of her own. Cassie's voice was a low whisper, questioning, wondering.

'Venetia . . .?'

'Silence!' snapped Levigny. 'Brother Bastien, bring the ceremonial knife.'

Suddenly there was something in Venetia's hand. She looked down at it. It was a silver dagger, her fingers curling automatically around its jewelled hilt. She stared at it in horror, wanting to let it go, but her fingers would not unlock; and there was a voice in her head, whispering do it, do it, do it now.

'Do it now, Venetia,' commented Levigny.

She turned to face him, questioning, afraid.

'I don't understand. What do you want me to do?'

'It is quite simple, Venetia. You are going to kill your sister.'

'No!'

Her scream bounced off the walls, ricocheting back as a terror-stricken echo.

'No, I won't do it. You're insane . . . let me go!'

Strong hands were on hers. Defarge's fingers were closing about hers, forcing the dagger closer and closer to the valley between Cassie's naked breasts.

'You must do it, Venetia. For the ritual of conjuration to work, sister must kill sister, like must slay like . . .'

'No . . .'

She had no strength to resist Defarge. He was a brute animal, a creature of raw evil, and he was overpowering her, forcing her to do that which her soul could never bear.

'Feel it, Brothers! Feel the power, it is all around us!'

They looked at each other, their faces distorting with lascivious glee.

'It is working!' cried Gérard.

Bastien smiled.

'The conjuration is taking effect already. The ancient spirits are joining with us in our worship.'

What happened next, happened so quickly that Venetia could scarcely begin to understand it. One minute she was standing over Cassie, the tip of a silver dagger poised only inches above her skin; the next, the whole Temple seemed to be shaking itself to bits.

'What's happening!' cried Venetia, but no one could hear her above the roar of the immense wind which tore through the subterranean chamber. 'For pity's sake, someone tell me what's happening . . .'

An icy wind was whirling and raging through

the chamber, violent as a hurricane, its power so great that Levigny was forced to his knees, and Venetia saw Léonore, eyes wide with terror, clutching at one of the marble pillars as the wind tried to claw her away.

Defarge alone stood against the blast, his hands upraised, his head thrown back. He was laughing, laughing like a madman.

'The spirits,' he roared. 'The spirits are here. Let us welcome them.'

But Venetia knew this could not be the way Levigny had planned it. His face was a mask of terror, his fingers clawing for holds on the smooth floor as the wind sucked and raked his bare flesh.

Fingers and lips blue and cold, Venetia fought to stay upright as she tried desperately to free her sister from the chains which held her fast to the altar. By some strange quirk of fate, she seemed to have a greater resistance to this curious, astral wind than the Brotherhood. It seemed almost as if it had not come for her, was not even interested in her. What it wanted was the Elect . . .

She heard Cassie's voice above the howling wind, and her fingers tightened about Venetia's wrist.

'Leave me. Run, Venetia, run!'

'No, never! I won't leave you.'

'Go, Venetia. They won't harm me, not if you have gone. Don't you see? They need both of us for their stupid ritual to work. *Both of us.* For

God's sake, go, get help . . .'

The wind was tugging at Venetia, pulling her away, almost as if it were directing her. Bastien reached out, trying to catch at her ankle as he lay on the ground, but she kicked his hand away with surprising ease. It was as if something, some unseen force, were helping her . . .

Venetia struggled from the central chamber, seizing a lantern and running, running, running down a rough-hewn passageway. She had no idea how she was going to escape, no idea of where she was heading; only knowing that somehow, she had to get to Esteban.

It was night. Deep, dark, moonless night.

Venetia had no way of knowing what time it was, or even what day it was, when she emerged from the secret passageway and into the twelfth-century church of St Agnès.

She was naked, afraid, and shivering with cold as she crossed the nave and left by the west door. Outside, stars shimmered in a placid sky of flawless matt black. She was completely, utterly alone.

And then she saw Bastien's car, the showy silver Mercedes she'd been foolish enough to get into that day on the coast road when the Citroën had broken down. Had he engineered that incident, got someone to tamper with the car and made sure he was in the right place at the right time? With hindsight, it seemed obvious that he had.

She was in luck. Bastien Le Rocq was careless with his possessions – but then again, he could afford to be. The car door was locked but the window was open and it wasn't difficult to reach inside and open it. She opened the glove-compartment and, sure enough, there they were, just where she remembered them being – Bastien's spare set of car keys.

Thanking her lucky stars, she fumbled the key into the lock and turned it. The engine sprang into life and she wasted no time in swinging the Mercedes on to the main road out of Valazur.

Every instinct in her body screamed to get out of here, to get as far away from Valazur as possible and never, ever come back. But it wasn't just her any more, was it? It was Cassie. Cassie was in mortal danger and if Venetia didn't do anything about it, who would?

She turned on to the coast road and pointed the car in the direction of Esteban's villa. Maybe she was being stupid yet again; maybe Esteban was in this too, and he would hand her back to Levigny and Defarge. Maybe. And yet . . .

And yet, she had to trust her instincts. Her instincts told her that Esteban was the only man who could help her.

The rest of the world might be asleep, but Venetia saw that a light was shining from a downstairs room in Esteban's villa as the gates swung open and she drove up towards the house. What was she going to say? And how was Esteban going to react to the arrival of a naked woman on his doorstep – a naked woman he'd told to get out of his life and never come back?

To her surprise the front door of the house was standing ajar. Tentatively she pushed it open and walked in, following the line of oil-lamps to the light emanating from Esteban's study. Pain filled her as she remembered that one, sublime night they had spent together, locked in each other's arms. She had thought then that it would never end, that the power of the attraction between them was too great to break.

And she remembered his caresses, his kisses; the feel of his lips on hers, possessing her, filling her with an intensity of pleasure that she had never known before and would never know again. Such kisses. He could so easily have made her a slave to his kiss. But instead, inexplicably, he had cast her off.

She had thought . . . she had been so very sure . . . but that had been an eternity ago.

Venetia stepped into Esteban's study. He was sitting in an armchair beside the fire, his hair dark and glossy against his pale face, his dark eyes glittering. All the old feelings came back as he turned those eyes upon her. And for a moment she thought she saw a look of pain cross his face.

He stood up, He was more beautiful than ever in his full-sleeved white shirt and close-fitting trousers of black leather.

'I told you to leave Valazur, Venetia. You would not listen to me.'

'Esteban. Oh Esteban, please, you have to help me.' She clutched at his arm but he half-turned away, as though he could not bear to meet her gaze. 'The Elect have got Cassie ... Bastien kidnapped me but I escaped ... you have to help me.'

'I ... I cannot.'

She forced him to look at her.

'You can, Esteban, I know you can.' A tear escaped from her brimming eyes. 'Why won't you do anything to help me, Esteban? Why? Are you going to hand me back to Levigny and Defarge, is that it?'

'That is something I would never do.'

'Then why didn't you tell me about them? You could have warned me about what was going on.'

'Would you have left Valazur if I had?'

'No, but . . .'

'There are some things that have to be learned, Venetia. It was really the only way. I warned you to leave. If was your decision to ignore my advice.'

Venetia rounded on him.

'You're an arrogant pig, Esteban, do you know that? An arrogant pig who only cares about himself and who uses people – like you used me. Or have you forgotten that letter you sent me? If you wanted to rid yourself of me, you could have had the decency to tell me to my face.'

'It was necessary,' said Esteban quietly.

'Necessary? *Necessary?* What's that supposed to mean?'

'It means that I had my reasons for ending something that should never have begun.'

Venetia's façade of anger was weakening with every moment she spent in this room with Esteban. Why had she come here? She should have known he cared nothing for her, known that once he had sated his physical hunger for her he would want to forget about her, pass on to his next conquest. But that wasn't what she had felt, and if she was honest it wasn't what she felt now, either. Could her instincts really have been so mistaken? Ruthlessly, she rubbed the beginnings of a tear from the corner of her eye.

'I think I'd better go. It was obviously a big mistake, my coming here. If you can just find me something to wear, anything, I'll get out of this place and never bother you again.'

She turned, but felt Esteban's hand on her shoulder.

'Stay. I have something to say to you.'

She swung round.

'Well?'

'What we had, Venetia . . . what we did. That

161

was something which I had sworn to deny myself, the moment I first saw you.' His fingers brushed her cheek lightly. 'I have my reasons, Venetia, it is better that I say no more.'

'Better? Who for, Esteban – for you? Tell me. You owe me that much. Tell me why.'

He turned the full force of his gaze upon her, and the powerful spell of his sexuality held her once more, transfixed.

'Because, Venetia . . .' He took a deep breath. 'Because I am a vampire.'

Chapter Eight

'WHAT!'

Venetia took a step back, not sure whether to be shocked or insulted.

'You heard what I said, Venetia.'

'And you seriously expect me to believe that, do you? That you're a *vampire*? What is this, some kind of sick joke?'

'I wish it were. But believe me, I have no interest in lying to you.'

Esteban paced the study floor like a caged animal, his fingers clenching and unclenching as though he were wrestling with some insoluble inner dilemma.

Venetia sank on to a chair, her legs suddenly very weak. All at once she felt terribly cold, her skin white and shivery . . .

'Let's take this slowly,' she said. 'Really slowly. Tell me again . . . what you just said.'

Esteban turned round to confront her. His face was white and drawn, pallid and almost ghostly in the light from the oil lamps. The look in his eyes made Venetia inexplicably afraid. It was a look of desperate hunger.

'I had vowed to hide this from you,' he said softly. 'I have hidden it for the world for seven centuries and more.'

'Seven . . .?'

Esteban raised his hand to silence her.

'No, listen to me. Let me speak. Afterwards, you may judge whether or not what I say is the truth.

Venetia watched him in stunned silence, her eyes following him as he paced the room.

'Seven hundred years ago, I was a crusader knight – a Castilian, sent to France to serve the Church and wipe out heresy.' He gave a hollow laugh. 'Such piety I had – it seems little better than a young man's foolishness now.' His eyes met Venetia's, and for a moment she saw a flicker of humour in their dark depths. 'I was arrogant then, too, Venetia. I thought I knew everything, but I knew nothing. Nothing at all. And my ignorance was my undoing.

'In those days, there were many religious and magical sects in southern France – Albigensians,

Flagellants, all manner of strange heresies. In Valazur there was an ancient cult of Gnosticism, brought here by the Romans in the first century AD. But it had changed from the original purity and piety of its founders. It had become something else – something corrupt which used black arts to fuel its power; something which delighted in the power of pain.

'I fought many battles.' Esteban unbuttoned his shirt cuff and pushed up the sleeve, revealing a long, white scar which ran from wrist to above the elbow. 'And I received many wounds. But none so deep or so painful as the wound inflicted upon me by the Gnostics of Valazur.'

Venetia stared at him, puzzled, unsure whether she could allow herself to believe a single word of what Esteban was saying. And yet he spoke with such conviction, such bitter sorrow.

'Esteban . . .' she began. 'I don't understand any of this. It's like something out of a dream . . .'

Esteban gave a dry laugh.

'A nightmare, Venetia. This is my nightmare and I must live it for ever.' He went over to the window, drew the curtain aside and looked out into the night. A few, far-off lights twinkled in the darkness at the other side of the bay, and somewhere in the distance Venetia could hear the soft splash, splash, splash of water lapping at the shore. 'All I ask of you is that you listen to what I have to say.'

'I'm listening, Esteban. But please don't ask me to believe.'

Without turning round, Esteban continued speaking. Venetia saw his knuckles whitening as his fingers gripped the stone window sill.

'They captured me. They were going to punish me, they said, because of what I stood for, because of those of their number that I had killed in battle, the villages we had burned ... Oh Venetia, I was not proud of the innocents who had perished with the guilty, at my hand; but I was proud, proud indeed, of the all-consuming, purifying fire which would rid this land of blackest heresy for all time.

'But now I was their captive, and I had no power against their black arts, not then. I thought the worst that they could do to me was torture and kill me; and I was not afraid either of pain or death. What an arrogant young fool I was.

'As you see, they did not kill me, Venetia. They did far worse than that. They cursed me to live on, throughout all eternity, as a vampire.'

Venetia shook her head, trying to rid it of the dark thoughts crowding into her brain.

'No, no, that's not possible. I'm dreaming this. Vampires ... for God's sake, Esteban, vampires don't exist!'

Esteban strode over, seized her chin and forced her to look up into hs face.

'That's right, Venetia. Vampires don't exist.'

He swung round and pulled open a drawer of his desk. Inside lay the little silver dagger he had used to slit through the lace of her panties, on that one night of shared passion. It seemed so long ago now, as though it had belonged to a different world, a different life.

Esteban took hold of it and lifted it up so that it caught the light, and flashed many-coloured fire from its jewelled handle.

'I don't exist, Venetia. Remember that, I don't exist.'

To her horror, he ripped open his shirt and pressed the blade of dagger against his skin, suddenly running it down his chest in a single, savage stroke which opened up the flesh in a long, deep cut.

'Esteban – no! What are you doing?'

Venetia leapt forward, trying to stem the flow of blood from the wound. It was pouring, oozing, welling up from the cut veins, its dark crimson life-force covering her hands, her naked skin.

Expressionless, Esteban looked down at the dagger, then let it fall to the stone floor with a clatter. Gently he pushed Venetia away, her hands and breasts bloody in the lamplight.

'I don't exist,' he whispered; and that whisper was filled with desolation.

As Venetia watched, the impossible began to happen. The bleeding began to stop, and the deep cut which led from the base of Esteban's throat to just above his navel started to close up, right before her eyes. One moment it was a bloody, jagged gash, the next it was a healing scar – and drop by drop, even the blood began to disappear, as though washed away by some unseen hand.

Until, within no longer than the space of a minute, there was not the slightest sign that Esteban's skin had ever been pierced – no cut, no blood, no scar. Nothing.

Venetia raised her hands to touch Esteban's skin and saw that even the blood on her own hands and breasts seemed to have evaporated, disappeared completely as if it had never been. Staring at her hands, she lifted them to Esteban's chest, running them over the flesh, flawed only by the ancient sword-scar.

'Oh Esteban, wake me. I'm dreaming. This just isn't real.' Her eyes beseeched him. 'Tell me it isn't true.'

Esteban lifted her hands away from his skin, almost as though he were afraid of her touch, afraid of the powerful emotions and sensations it awakened within him.

'It is true, Venetia. I am invulnerable. I cannot die, I cannot age, I can never escape from the curse which was placed upon me.' He returned her gaze steadily, enunciating his words with a conscious brutality. 'You must try to understand. If the hunger came upon me now, I could drain the blood from your fragile body and you would be powerless to stop me.'

'No, Esteban, no!'

'I could end your frail existence with a single, bloody kiss.'

Venetia stared at him, filled with a mixture of horror and pity and a desire which she could not repress, no matter how hard she tried.

'You have ... you have done it before.' It wasn't a question, it was a statement.

'When the hunger rages through my body, the pain ... oh Venetia, I cannot tell you of the pain. I can suppress it for a little while, find ways of resisting. But sooner or later, I must feed.'

'Peterson.' Venetia's breath escaped in a gasp of realisation. 'It was you ... it must have been.'

'He was nothing.'

'How can you say that!' Venetia's eyes flashed anger. 'You killed him, and you have the nerve to stand there and say he was nothing!'

'I had no choice. He was unlucky. He stumbled upon the truth about me at the very moment when my hunger was at its most intense.' Esteban ran his slender fingers through his glossy black hair. He looked drawn, exhausted. 'Now do you see why it could never be, why I had to force you to leave this place and never come back again?

'Have you any idea, the remotest understanding of the torments I feel ... the hunger that burns within me? Do you realise how much danger you are in, each moment you remain here with me? Go, Venetia. Get out of here, leave me now, before it is too late.'

Venetia's head was spinning, her thoughts making no sense. But one truth stood out above and beyond everything that Esteban had said.

'I came here to ask you for your help,' she said. 'To beg for it if necessary. Cassie is in danger – the Elect have her and they are going to sacrifice us both if they catch me again. I believe that you can help us, Esteban. I *know* that you can. You *have* to help us.'

'I do not have to do anything.'

'For pity's sake, Esteban! If you don't care about me, or Cassie, or anything else, you've already told me how much you hate the Elect for what they did to you!'

'I hated them once,' Esteban conceded. 'But then they were genuinely powerful, I almost respected them for their learned evil, their sophisticated corruption. But now . . .' His lips curled into a contemptuous sneer.

'Now? What has changed, Esteban? They are still evil.'

'They are weak men, playing at evil,' snapped Esteban. 'They are not worthy adversaries; they are not even worthy of my contempt.'

Her anger and her pain greater by far than her fear, Venetia seized him by the arms, forced him to acknowledge her.

'You could destroy them, Esteban. I know you

could. You could destroy them and help me to rescue Cassie.'

'Perhaps. Perhaps not.'

'You could, and yet you will not. Why, Esteban? Why?'

'I have told you, Venetia. I care for nothing, for no one.'

'Not even for Cassie, alone and afraid?'

'No.'

'Not even for your own self-respect?'

Esteban caught her hand and, quite suddenly, drew it to his lips, kissing it with an unexpected tenderness.

'There is a great passion within you, Venetia Fellowes. But you have no understanding. Any self-respect I had, I lost seven hundred years ago, and it will never return.'

Venetia was silent for a few moments, her mind and body in turmoil, fighting a losing battle against the flood of sensations which washed over her as Esteban's lips touched her fingertips. This was madness, that much was obvious. She had seen with her own eyes the insane power within Esteban. But he was like a drug to her, the force of his sensuality overwhelming her, drawing her in as a spider lures a fly, tempting her so that even the fear of death was not enough to quell the terrible wanting within her.

'If you do not care for Cassie, or for yourself,' she told him, 'what about me? Tell me that you feel nothing for me, Esteban, and I will go. Swear to me that you do not want me . . .'

Her hands caressed his face and slowly, very slowly, she drew his head down until their lips were only a breath apart.

'No, Venetia,' whispered Esteban, but he did not push her away.

'I want you, Esteban. And I know you want me too.'

They kissed. It was Venetia who initiated the embrace, her lips first brushing his hesitantly, lightly, the trembling of her own body transmitting itself to his. And then Esteban began to respond, his lips crushing hard against hers, his hands clutching at her, pulling her towards him, capturing her in an inescapable embrace.

Venetia did not know what had overcome her, could not understand how her desire could be stronger than her fear. All she knew was that she wanted Esteban with every fibre of her being, that her whole body ached and tingled with the need for release, her own deep, dark hunger which could never leave her until it had been sated.

She tore at his already ripped shirt with fingers grown clumsy with excitement, pulling and tugging it down over his shoulders, kissing him again and again; now on the mouth, now on the throat, the chest, the belly.

Esteban ran his fingers down her neck and back, clawing and scratching with a sensual skill which drove her wild with lust. His back was arched, leaning against the desk where, in the one night of passion they had shared, he had so roughly and so passionately taken Venetia's willing gift of lust.

Now she was demanding that gift for herself, her kisses and caresses pleading with him to offer up the honesty of his own lust. And he could no longer resist, his resolve crumbling, his body leading him where he had sworn he would never go. Not with Venetia . . .

Venetia's lips closed about Esteban's nipple and she felt him shiver at the touch. It was a small, dark button of flesh, a dusky coffee-colour against his paler skin. As her mouth explored it, the slightly concave disc began to swell and harden into a stiff, rubbery teat; a peak whose very summit was so sensitive that it responded instantly to the soft, wet flick of her tongue.

The fingers of her right hand began toying with Esteban's left nipple and this dual caress so excited him that his fingernails began digging deep into the flesh of Venetia's back, running up and down, leaving white claw-marks which quickly reddened into long, raised weals.

Venetia moaned softly as her teeth tormented Esteban's nipple. They were two wild animals now, all semblance of tender humanity forgotten as they explored each other's bodies with a reckless hunger.

She slid down her hand to unfasten Esteban's belt, but he had anticipated her desire and his fingers were already unbuckling it, the silver buckle clinking as it yielded to his will. Venetia knew what she longed to do and, allowing his nipple to escape from her mouth, she slid to her knees, leaving a long trail of kisses down her lover's belly.

Esteban had already unfastened the top button of his black leather trousers, but the fly was still fastened tightly across the long, hard swell of his penis, with a row of five metal buttons, His erection lay diagonally across the base of its belly, its outline clearly moulded by the skin-tight leather and its swollen tip only a fraction beneath the level of the waistband.

His testes were pushed to one side by the tight crotch of the trousers, and they formed a deliciously plump bulge to the right of his cock, firm and juicy and begging for release.

It was as though desire had sharpened her senses, for she could smell the familiar spicy scent of his desire, and could almost taste it on her tongue as she closed her eyes and kissed the long swelling beneath his trousers. She experimented by biting his cock, very gently, through the leather, and felt him harden still further.

'Ma chère petite, ma chère petite, je n'en puis plus . . .'

But Venetia knew that he *could* bear it, and

more; just as she could bear the burning wet sensation between her bare thighs. She longed for the fragrance of her coupling with Esteban.

She took the first fly-button between her teeth and felt for the cotton thread holding it in place. It was resilient, but her teeth were sharp and strong, and with a single, scything bite she tore the button loose.

Esteban's trousers parted just a little more, and for the first time since their night of shared pleasure, Venetia glimpsed the glossy, pierced head of his dick, pushing its way out from beneath the tight black leather sheath.

Oh, how she wanted him. She could scarcely believe how much. She wasn't a silly young girl, but she knew she had lost all sense of reason when it came to Esteban. She had even forgotten, momentarily, the reason why she had come here. The only thing that seemed to matter, here and now, was the power of the sensations passing between them.

Esteban was breathing heavily, moving his pelvis to meet the caress of her lips, and she did not need him to tell her that he felt the same power that was surging through her. She had not even kissed his dick yet; had not even felt his fingers stroking across the forested mound of her pubis – yet she felt so close to coming that her entire body was quivering with anticipation.

The second button yielded, more easily than

the first, and then the third. Now she could see the black curls leading in a thin line from his navel to the roof of his penis. His cock lay to one side, coyly hiding itself from her kisses as she pressed her face to his belly and let her tongue explore the fragrance of his sex.

He reached down and released the remaining two buttons, and his cock sprang out of its prison, nuzzling its pink muzzle against her cheek, dripping salty wetness on to her eager lips.

Venetia pulled down Esteban's trousers, tugging them down over his hips, his thighs, baring the beauty of his nakedness. His balls were heavy and ripe, and their wrinkled purse of flesh tensed appreciatively at her touch. She undressed him with an impatient hunger, and he stepped out of them, kicking them to one side.

Barefoot and naked, he stood before her, his cock pressing against her mouth.

'Now. Do it now,' he breathed, taking hold of his prick and pushing its tip against her mouth.

She put out her tongue and lapped at the tip of Esteban's penis. It was slippery-wet, salty-smooth, its juices warm and delicious.

'You have such a beautiful prick,' she murmured. 'I want to take it inside me . . . in my mouth, my sex. I want you to masturbate over my face, my breasts, my belly . . .'

She sucked the very tip of Esteban's prick, pushing her tongue-tip into the tiny, weeping eye of his glans, delighting in the taste and texture of his sex.

'Venetia . . . Venetia, you torture me . . .'

Esteban curled his fingers around his shaft and, as Venetia licked his glans, he began to masturbate, his left hand stroking the long golden mane of her hair.

'If you knew,' he whispered, his face contorted in ecstatic agony. 'If you knew the hunger that burns in me for you.'

Or the hunger that is in me for you, thought Venetia to herself. For nothing could be more powerful than the burning in her clitoris, the sweet torture of her empty sex. Never had any man made her feel the way Esteban did. And she knew that no other man would, ever again. This night was precious and irreplaceable, its urgency heightened by the piquant agony of fear.

Esteban's foreskin slid back and forth, now hiding his glans, now exposing it like some purple plum, running with juice. Venetia licked it all away, kissing the pleasure from him, sharing his arousal as he brought himself towards orgasm. His balls were so heavy, so tempting; and her fingers strayed to caress them, gently rubbing and stroking them inside their loose, fleshy sac.

She knew he was about to spurt, perhaps even before he did. She felt the tensing of his balls, the gradual swelling of his shaft, saw the deepening purple of his glans and felt the pulsing of the veins on the underside of his penis.

And then, suddenly, his prick was jerking and his seed was spattering her face, her throat, her breasts, even her hair; great white jets of it spurting out, forming shiny, pearly patches of wetness all over her skin.

'Venetia . . .' He gasped his pleasure as the last trickles of seed oozed from his cock-tip.

He swayed a little, momentarily weakened after the force of his passion, and Venetia drew him down until they were lying, side by side, on the cool stone floor.

They kissed, and the wetness of semen smeared over their flesh, a symbol of their shared passion.

'Like me,' she said. 'I want you to taste your own pleasure.'

'I want to taste *your* pleasure,' he replied, kissing the wet semen from her eyelids, her cheeks, her lips. 'I want to feel it on my face, I want it to trickle into my mouth. I want to drink it down. I want you to give me your beautiful pussy to kiss, Venetia? Will you let me?'

Venetia's heart missed a beat. The thought of Esteban's kisses on her sex both terrified and aroused her.

'I . . .'

Esteban rolled on to his back, his hair spread out behind his head like a dark halo.

'Trust me, Venetia,' he said.

His eyes burned into hers, and suddenly she heard himself whispering: 'I do trust you, Esteban. I do.'

He lay on his back beneath her, and she knelt astride his face, her sex only inches above his lips.

'Lower yourself on to me, Venetia. I hunger for you.'

No, no, she couldn't. She couldn't let him. She wanted to pull away, but she wanted just as much to let him do whatever he wanted to her. Oh, how her sex burned for him, how her body ached for his kisses and caresses.

She felt his hands on her thighs, pulling her down, and she yielded, at first trembling with fear, then with delicious anticipation as she felt his lips pressing softly against the flesh of her parted labia.

'You are so beautiful,' he murmured. 'So beautiful, I could kiss you for ever.'

The first touch of his tongue on her inner sex was a revelation of sheer, exquisite pleasure. The thrill ran through her, the excitement swelling her clitoris as Esteban's tongue-tip crept closer and closer to the heart of her need.

She flung back her head, eyes closed, needing nothing more than the world of sound and scent and sensation. The warm summer night was filled with the scents of passion, the oozing, trickling, gushing stream of her pleasure, dropping on to Esteban's tongue as he held apart the flower of her sex.

This must surely be paradise, this mingling of passion, this ecstatic meeting of bodies so compatible that they needed no words, only the language of touch and caress. Venetia's only sounds were wordless, formless moans of utter helplessness as, little by little, the last barriers of her resistance melted away, leaving only the complete liberation of sexual ecstasy.

He held her fast as she came, drinking down every drop of the clear, sweet juice which gushed from the well-spring of her sex. His tongue prolonged the pleasure, darting into the deep cavern of her vagina and holding her there for what seemed forever, before at last freeing her, letting the last, irresistible spasms ebb and die away.

Her sex singing with need, she slid down Esteban's body until she was astride his hips. She bent to kiss him and his hands seized her roughly impaling her upon the upraised staff of his swollen penis.

'Esteban, Esteban, oh . . .!' She gave a shriek of excitement as his pierced cock slid right up into her, so deeply that his cock-ring pushed against her cervix, provoking powerful waves of sensation.

'Ride me, *chère* Venetia,' commanded Esteban, his eyes closing in ecstasy as his hips began to buck and thrust. 'Ride me and never, ever stop.'

*

The night was velvet-black, the sky dotted with tiny pinpricks of light. On the grass in front of the villa, Esteban and Venetia lay entwined, oblivious to the chill of the darkness which would soon become dawn.

'I will help you,' said Esteban, stroking Venetia's hair as she lay with her head on his chest.

She raised herself on one arm, looking into the glittering black diamonds of his eyes.

'You mean it? You will help me rescue Cassie?'

'I always mean what I say,' replied Esteban. 'Yes, I will help you and Cassandra. But you must understand, there will be a price to pay in exchange. A price which, I fear, you will not be willing to pay.'

'Anything,' said Venetia firmly. 'I will do anything to help my sister.'

'Yes,' said Esteban softly, almost distantly. Then he looked deep into her eyes again. 'Listen to me, Venetia. Seven hundred years I have been alone in my pain. I have met many beautiful women, but never . . .' He stroked Venetia's breast. 'Never one like you.'

'Please, Esteban, explain.'

'Very well, Venetia. I will help you, but only on my terms: your soul for Cassandra's safety. If you wish me to help save your sister, you must agree to become a vampire.'

Chapter Nine

THE FIRST GLIMMERINGS of dawn were paling the eastern sky, turning midnight-black to a rich spectrum of cobalt blue, apricot, rose-pink and deepest, fiery orange.

Esteban stood by the bedroom window, looking out at the gathering dawn, the light shimmering over the distant sea.

'I must leave you now.' He turned towards Venetia, curled up on the four-poster bed, her skin pale and lustrous in the last rays of the dying moon.

'But Esteban.' A note of desperation caught in Venetia's throat, her mouth dry, the pain of memory returning. 'What about Cassie?'

Stooping over the bed, Esteban took her face

between his hands and kissed her parted lips.

'Remember, Venetia. Remember what I said.'

'I can't believe it, Esteban, I cannot. It seems like some crazy dream. You didn't mean what you said, you can't have done.'

'I told you, *ma chère*. I never say what I do not mean. If you wish me to help you, once I have returned your sister safely to you, you must pay my price.'

The cold hand of fear stroked its icy fingers over Venetia's bare skin, dug its frozen nails into her heart.

'A vampire,' she whispered. 'To become a vampire . . . for ever . . .'

'For ever, Venetia. Make no mistake. There is no cure, no escape, no going back. If you accept my bargain you will be alone with me throughout eternity.'

'And if I do not?'

He turned his face away, so that it was half-hidden by shadow, half-illuminated by the pinkish-orange light from the open window. He looked for all the world like a statue of some seductive demon, or some beautiful bird of prey, his eyes reduced to glittering points of light in a shadowy face.

'Then I cannot be responsible for what happens to your sister.' He glanced at Venetia. 'Or to you, my sweet.'

His fingers sought out hers, and they interlaced, his grip strong and almost desperate.

'Say that you will accept, Venetia.'

'You are blackmailing me, Esteban.' Venetia's voice was pleading with him now, all her anger gone, only the fear remaining. Not just the fear of what might be to come, but also the fear of herself – of the overwhelming attraction which she felt to this man, this sensual creature, this arrogantly beautiful vampire.

'As you will.'

'Don't do this to me, Esteban!' She kissed him, her fingers running through his dark hair, her lips hot and moist on his cool cheek. 'If there is any humanity left in you . . .'

'There is none.'

Esteban's voice was husky, very quiet. Venetia wished that she could see his face, but in the twilight of dawn it was an expressionless mask. Could he truly be as emotionless and inhumane as he claimed to be? Why then did she feel this overpowering sense of desire towards him? Why did he not repulse her, make her want to run away and never look back? She wished that she could understand the emotions and sensations he awakened in here.

'That is your last word, Esteban? You will not soften your heart to me?'

He whispered his reply, and his voice sounded eerie in the silence: 'I have spoken.'

There was a long pause, punctuated only by the

regular tick, tick, tick of an unseen clock, counting away the seconds until eternity.

'I accept, Esteban. For Cassie's sake, I accept. Don't fail me, please don't fail me, Esteban. If this is some kind of trick . . .'

The words tore from her as though icy fingers were ripping her heart from her chest, the pain extreme, and yet the sense of release extraordinarily liberating.

He kissed her fingers, pressing them to his lips, caressing them with his tongue. There was real passion in his kisses, as though they were his only way of convincing her that he spoke the truth.

'You have my word, Venetia. I can offer you no other proof of my honesty.'

He stood up. She saw him silhouetted against the window, his body tall and slender and hard-muscled, his cock still swollen and standing proud, its tip glistening in the dawn light. In that moment she desired him all over again, felt once more the full force of the lust which had transfixed and overwhelmed her, the very first time their eyes had met.

'Stay with me, Esteban, don't go.'

'I must. It is almost day.'

'You mean you can't . . .?' Confused images whirled and spun in Venetia's head. Vampires . . . horror-movie monsters who hid from the daylight, lest it destroy them, making them crumble into dust. If she became a vampire, would that happen to her, too?

Esteban anticipated her question and parried it with soft, warm laughter.

'You should not believe *everything* you see at the movies, *ma chère,*' he chuckled. 'It is true that I shun the light of day, for the full glare of the sun pains and weakens me. That is why I walk by night, and make my living in the casinos. But no, my sweet vixen, the sunlight cannot destroy me. Nothing can destroy me, and that is the tragedy of my wasted existence.'

He paused, as though his own words had transported him far back in history, to a time before he had been cursed to immortality.

'You must sleep now,' he told Venetia, forcing himself back to the immediacy of the moment. 'You will need your strength for what is to come. At dusk we will go together to Valazur, and pay a visit to Gérard's Bar . . .'

'The bar?' Venetia was puzzled. 'But they are holding Cassie in their underground temple . . .'

Esteban shook his head.

'I have certain telepathic powers,' he explained. 'You will have to trust me. The Elect have taken her to the bar. Levigny believes no one will think of looking there. But they are fools, all of them. Poor, ignorant, deluded fools.'

He bent over the bed, and his caresses were cool and gentle as a night breeze, wafting over her nakedness, soothing her, making her feel drowsy and relaxed and drifting, drifting, so close to sleep. His lips brushed the skin of her throat, and for a moment Venetia wondered if his professed honesty had all been a sham, if in this moment of her complete vulnerability he was about to take from her what she had promised him in return for his help. She shivered, half in fear, half in sweetly wicked temptation.

'Sleep now,' he whispered. And when she opened her eyes again, he had gone, leaving a rose beside her on her pillow.

She reached out to caress its dew-fresh petals, but as her fingers touched it, it withered before her eyes, turning to a fine, powdery dust.

As the sun rose over Valazur, Venetia slept. Her dreams were all of Esteban, of the stirring of desire within her and the passion that seared and burned and yearned for release.

In her dreams they lay together on the beach, the sand white and burning beneath their naked bodies and the sun a golden orb of flame in a sky of deepest blue.

The tide was coming in, thin fingers and tongues of water creeping up the ribbed sea-shore to lap and stroke their bodies as they coupled. They lay on their sides, Venetia's backside moulding perfectly into the hollow formed by Esteban's belly and thighs, one of his hands on her hip and the other beneath her, stroking the underside of her breast.

A trickle of wetness was seeping out of her on to the burning heat of the dry, white sand. Esteban's penis was sliding down the deep crevasse of her backside, leaving a trail of its own slick wetness as it searched out the heart of her need.

She welcomed him in with a little cry of passion, her buttocks thrusting out to meet him and accepting the knife-thrust of his dick as he penetrated the flower of her sex. She blossomed for him, her soft pink petals opening wide and her nectar oozing, sticky and sweet, about the stamen of his manhood.

'Venetia, Venetia . . .'

She could hear his voice in each wave of the sea as it crept up the beach, each swish and crash of the snowy-white breakers, riding high on the waves of crystal blue. The oily sea ebbed and flowed, with each new wave creeping nearer, touching and embracing their bodies, begging with them to join their passion to the eternal, ever-renewing passion of the wild ocean.

Seabirds cried above them, their white bodies flashing through the sunlit sky, their wings outspread, crying for the sheer joy of their freedom. And Esteban and Venetia coupled in a blessed torment of ecstasy, each tiny movement bringing with it a new delight, a new torture of frustrated hunger.

They were moving more quickly now, their passion moving inexorably towards its crisis, their hips thrusting harder as their hunger overtook them and the last of Venetia's self-control ebbed away. Esteban held her fast in his embrace, stroking and pinching her flesh, holding her hips and pulling them back, hard on to the shaft of his cock. Oh, the deep, dark pleasure of it as she felt his cock-ring nudge again and again against her g-spot, taking her far beyond the realms of human pleasure, and into a world where pleasure would never end.

'Take me, take me,' she heard herself murmur, an urgent gasp of pleasure.

'Come, Venetia. Let me make you come.'

'Take me . . . oh Esteban, take me. Can't you feel it? I'm coming, coming, coming . . .'

Orgasm overwhelmed her, shook her like a rag doll, robbed her of the last, tenuous thread of control. She was an elemental creature now, no longer human; a being made from pure pleasure, for whom pleasure alone was the reason for existence.

Esteban was pumping into her as the petals of her sex opened into the blossom of ecstasy, his creamy-white tide spurting out of him, jetting into her, taking her to the heights of purest delight and far, far beyond.

'*Chère* Venetia,' she heard him whisper as he kissed the nape of her neck, very tenderly, very gently. 'My darling, we shall be together forever.'

And as the first cold wave washed over their coupled bodies, she felt his lips press against her neck, and knew that soon, very soon, his sharp white teeth would pierce her virgin throat . . .

The shutters were closed, the sign turned to 'Fermé'. It was not yet dusk, but Gérard's Bar had not been open for business all day. Instead of Gérard's regular customers, the Elect were gathered in the bar, contemplating the naked body of their captive.

Cassie lay on her back on the polished bar-top, her wrists bounds behind her, unable to escape from the rough caresses lavished upon her helpless nakedness. Even her cries went unheard, for an inflatable rubber gag had been forced between her teeth; and all she could do was endure her captors' perverse desires.

She knew now what had happened to her. Seeing Venetia again had broken through the hypnotic trance of her servitude and reawakened her to the danger of her situation. She had grown up a lot since she had wandered unwarily into the arms of the Elect, all those weeks ago. And she had been listening to what they had said – their plans to use her and Venetia for some magical ritual in which one of them, at least, must die.

In all honesty, she could not blame Venetia if, having once escaped, she simply headed straight out of Valazur and never turned back. Over the years she had caused her sister nothing but trouble, with her sexual adventuring. If she ever got out of this alive, she would make it up to her, she had promised herself that she would.

'You should not have let Venetia escape,' hissed Defarge, his eyes narrowing to angry slits in his brutish face.

'If it had not been for the meddling of Esteban', retorted Bastien Le Rocq, 'she would still remain with us and we would be preparing for the sacred ritual tonight.'

'It may yet happen,' remarked Jean-Marc Levigny, calmly drawing the cork from a bottle of red wine and pouring himself a glass. He held it up to the light, examining its rich, ruby colour. Just like the colour of freshly shed blood. 'Esteban is an arrogant fool who thinks he knows everything, but knows nothing.'

'It was Esteban who caused the spirit-wind at the ritual?' asked Gérard. 'Esteban who caused the girl to escape? But why?'

Levigny sighed. Gérard was a loyal acolyte, but sometimes he wearied of the man's intellectual paucity.

'Because the girl has bewitched his senses.' He laughed. 'And we will bewitch them both, and lead them back to us and to their destruction.'

'How, Brother Jean-Marc?' demanded Bastien.

'Through Esteban's imagined cleverness,'

replied Levigny, drinking down his wine at a single gulp. It seemed to revive his senses, making his eyes bright as a bird's. 'I have made it known to him that Cassandra is here. He is bound to tell the Englishwoman, and she – through some misguided sense of loyalty – will come to claim her sister from us.'

'And what if Esteban comes with her? What if he agrees to help her?' demanded Defarge.

'He will not. Esteban cares only for his own gratification. Why should he help some silly English girl who has stumbled into his embrace? He will take his pleasure of her and then abandon her to us.'

'But if he *does* help her?' enquired Bastien. 'If he does come here with Venetia?'

'Then we shall destroy him,' replied Levigny with smug certainty. 'In fact, I should rather enjoy the opportunity to humiliate that arrogant upstart.'

He emptied the wine-bottle into four glasses then licked the last drops of blood-red fluid from the neck. It was a smooth, fat neck, plump and rounded and hard. He ran his fingers down it. It felt like an erect dick, hungry for prey. He glanced at Cassie, then at Defarge.

'Has she been thoroughly prepared for the ritual of conjuration?'

Defarge's face split into a leer of evil satisfaction. Cassie might not have her twin sister's spirit, but she was an arousing little filly in her own right; and now that she had awakened from her trance she had kicked and spat and bitten like a she-cat on heat.

'Brother Bastien and I have prepared her,' he replied.

'Good. All is as it should be.' Levigny's fingers caressed the neck of the bottle as he contemplated Cassie with a thoughtful smile. 'She will make a satisfactory vessel for our ritual. And once we have her sister too, the dark spirits we conjure shall make us the most powerful men on the Riviera. Powerful, wealthy, sexually irresistible . . .'

He set the empty wine-bottle down on the bar-top.

Dusk was falling as Venetia parked the car on the outskirts of Valazur and started walking into the centre of the village.

The place was deserted – unusual even for this small French village. On summer evenings there were always a few people strolling in the square, a few lovers kissing and laughing beside the fountain. But on this particular evening the place was as quiet as a ghost-town, nothing stirring, no sounds disturbing the silence save the plashing of the fountain and the distant chime of the clock at the *hôtel de ville*.

As she approached Gérard's Bar she could see

that it was in darkness, except for the glimmer of a single light behind the shuttered windows. Her heart raced, her pulse thumping so hard that the veins in her temples swelled and pulsated.

She tried to remember what Esteban had said: 'Trust me, I have given my word.' But how could she trust him after what he had made her promise? Could anyone trust a vampire's word? Was this all a crazy dream, and would she awake to discover herself in bed with Ramon in a tent near Istanbul?

Trust me. Trust me, Venetia.

She thought she heard Esteban's voice, whispering in the shadows of her fearful mind, but she shook the thought of him away. She knew what she must do, and she would not turn and run away, not now, even though the cold sweat of fear trickled down into the deep valley between her breasts.

Reaching the front door of the bar, she raised her fist; hesitated; then knocked.

A few seconds later, the door swung open on silent hinges, and she stepped into the darkness.

'So, *Mademoiselle* Venetia, you have decided to pay us a little visit? It is quite delightful to see you again so soon.'

In the dimly-lit bar, Jean-Marc Levigny lifted his glass to Venetia in an ironic toast of welcome.

Venetia stood her ground, though her entire

being screamed to her to run, to do anything, to scream and shout and try to escape. Anything to get away from here.

'I've come to get Cassie. Give my sister back to me.'

A ripple of subdued laughter ran around the assembled guests. Defarge stepped forward, his powerful frame menacing in the thin white robe he wore.

'Give her to me, Brother Jean-Marc. I will teach her humility.'

Jean-Marc Levigny smiled. A smile that was as cold and dark as his evil heart.

'Patience, Brother Luc. Soon, we shall all have an opportunity to teach *Mademoiselle* Venetia some valuable discipline. And she will learn so much from us. Isn't that so, *ma chère anglaise*?'

Levigny stroked Venetia's arm and she barely resisted the urge to take a step back, the rest of her bravery swiftly draining away. But she would not turn tail and run. Stubbornness lent her at least the semblance of courage. She had come this far, and she would not show her fear.

'My sister,' she repeated, this time louder and more resolutely.

'Ah yes, *chère enfant*. You have come to see your sister. Well, we shall not disappoint you, Venetia.' Levigny gave Bastien a court nod. 'Bring her forth, Brother Bastien.'

Bastien turned and walked through the

curtained doorway behind the bar. Venetia tried to follow, but Defarge seized her and held her back. She turned and snarled at him, with unaccustomed ferocity, 'Get your filthy hands off me!'

He seemed almost taken aback for a split second, then threw back his head and roared with laughter. 'What a joy it is to have an untrained filly, Brothers. And what a joy it will be to break her.'

With a rustling of the bead curtain, three figures stepped into the bar. First was Bastien, cold-eyed and sophisticated; then Léonore, her reddish-brown hair sweeping down her bare back in a single braid.

Between them walked the third figure: a golden-haired princess, naked and trembling, her pink nipples pierced and linked by a thin golden chain. Bastien was leading her with it, as one might lead an unwilling beast; and Venetia saw the fear in her sister's eyes.

'Cassie!' she gasped.

There was a single tear on Cassie's peachy-soft cheek. Her blue eyes met Venetia's.

'You should have run away,' Cassie whispered. 'You should have left me, saved yourself . . .'

'Never!' Venetia's eyes flashed cold fire. 'Let her go! Let my sister go, or I will . . .'

'Or what, Venetia?' enquired Bastien coolly. 'I think not, *chérie*. I think that you and Cassie will be staying with us. I think that, perhaps, you will never leave this place again.'

'Where is your lover, Venetia?' taunted Defarge. 'Where is your lover Esteban with all his fine promises?'

A voice, dark with menace, seemed to fill the entire room.

'I am here. Can you not see me? Can you not *feel* my presence among you?'

'Esteban!' gasped Venetia, wheeling round. But there was no one there. No one at all in the room except Cassie, Venetia, and the cult members.

Levigny's knuckles whitened as his hands tensed into fists. His eyes searched the room, a tinge of alarm in his voice, for all his bluster.

'This is some sort of trick, Brothers.'

'No trick,' replied Esteban. 'Unless it be the trick of your own fear. Can you feel how hot it is getting in here, Brothers? Can you feel the flames of hell licking at your bare flesh?'

'No ... no, it cannot be true.' Gérard was clawing at his throat, rivers of perspiration coursing down his brow. 'It cannot ...'

Bastien smiled, but he too could feel the heat, oppressive and suffocating, closing in, burning, searing.

'You can do nothing to us, Esteban. You are worthless, powerless against the might of the Elect.'

'I have waited many years for my revenge upon

you,' hissed Esteban. And suddenly he was standing beside Venetia, his dark eyes glittering a demonic menace.

'Such a piety,' retorted Levigny. 'For now that you are here, we really have no other option but to destroy you.'

'Really?' replied Esteban, a sneer in his voice as he raised his arms Heavenwards. 'You surprise me. You see, my dear Brothers, I have come to send you straight to Hell.'

Seconds later, a hot, suffocating blackness seemed to overcome Venetia, shutting out every glimmer of light, destroying everything except the fear, and the distant echo of Esteban's voice, whispering to her: 'Trust me, Venetia. Trust me, trust me.'

And then, all of a sudden, the whole world turned to flame.

'Venetia? Oh, Venetia, it's you! It's really you!'

Venetia opened her eyes to find herself sprawled naked on the roadside, opposite Gérard's Bar.

Or what had once been Gérard's Bar. Flames leapt fifty feet into the air, yellow and orange and red tongues licking and crackling against the deep blackness of the night sky. Nothing could survive an inferno like that. Nothing.

Perhaps not even Esteban.

Cassie was lying beside her, raising herself on

her arms to stare in wonder at the conflagration. Venetia embraced her, holding her so tightly that she almost crushed her with the sheer force of her love.

'Cassie, oh Cassie, you're safe! Everything's going to be all right now, I promise. Everything's going to be fine.'

And they sobbed together, sharing their happiness. But Venetia trembled for what had been, and the fear of what was yet to be.

A tall figure stood silhouetted against the horizon, gazing down on to the village of Valazur.

Gérard's bar was burning so fiercely that the flames had tinged the night sky pink, yet curiously the fire showed no sign of spreading to any other buildings. It would not. Esteban had planned it that way.

He watched for a few moments, satisfied with his work; then turned and walked away, wiping a dark trickle of blood from the corner of his sensual mouth.

Chapter Ten

CAPITAINE GUILLAUME BOILEAU, of the Nice fire service, tipped his helmet to the back of his head and scratched it reflectively.

'I just don't understand anything about this case,' he remarked, standing back and taking another look at the remains of Gérard's Bar. 'None of it makes sense.'

'It was probably arson,' volunteered Lieutenant Stanislaus, an attractive brunette who had been resisting the Captain's persistent sexual advances for a good six months now. He rather liked that sort of bloody-minded integrity in a woman. He'd probably have her promoted if her resolve held up. 'Lots of people had a grudge against Gérard Bellefeuille.'

'Possibly they did,' agreed Boileau. 'But there aren't any signs of deliberate fire-raising. No flammable substances, no frayed electrical cables. Nothing. Then again, there are all these sudden disappearances from the village at about the same time as the fire – Bellefeuille, Bastien and Léonore Le Rocq, Levigny, even Inspector Defarge. It's all very suspicious.'

'And then there's the other thing,' pointed out Stanislaus.

'What "other thing" would that be?'

'The locks, Captain.'

'What about them?'

'Every single door and window was locked from the inside, and there were half-filled wine-glasses on the bar. Yet there's no sign of anyone inside. It's like the Marie bloody Celeste in there.'

The night was dark, dark as the cold, black eternity which reached out its arms in a kiss of desolation.

Beneath the stars lay Esteban and Venetia, their bodies locked in a passion that knew no beginning, no end. If only this moment might last forever; if only she might hold it, cherish it, keep it unblemished and never awaken from the pleasure of its embrace.

Venetia lay beneath Esteban, his strong thighs astride her belly, a pearly trail of semen running between her breasts. Her body quivered and trembled in the afterglow of orgasm as he bent to lick and kiss her skin, reawakening the irresistible ache of her sexual hunger.

Something had passed between them in the silent darkness of the August night; something more than simple physical pleasure. It frightened Venetia in its intensity, robbing her of free will, enslaving her to the kisses of burning passion which he placed so tenderly upon her belly and her breasts.

He lay on top of her, his lips joined to hers, the mingled spice of their coupling exciting her again, again, again.

'No more, Esteban . . . please, no more.'

'We made a bargain, Venetia,' he whispered, and his lips caressed her eyelids, her cheek, her throat.

She opened her eyes and, taking his face between her hands, kissed him, pushing her tongue between his lips, possessing him in the way that he had possessed her. Could he feel it too? Was he, too, in the grip of this agony, this ecstasy of passion which ached and burned and would not let her be free?

Not that it mattered, not any more. After this night, she would never be free again.

'You kept your part of the bargain, Esteban,' she murmured, kissing him again.

He looked deep into her eyes, terrifying yet

thrilling her with the intensity of his passion.

'You are willing?'

'You kept your word. Now I must keep mine.'

He caressed her, his hands roaming over her nakedness, drinking in every sinuous curve, every ripe swell, every deep valley. When he spoke again, his voice was oddly devoid of expression, as though he were trying to suppress some dark and unwilling emotion.

'I am willing to free you from that word, Venetia.'

She drew back from his caresses, startled, even afraid.

'I . . . I don't understand, Esteban.'

'I told you, Venetia. I am willing to free you, to let you go. But listen to me, *ma chère*.' His hands clutched at her, his kisses passionate, almost violent. 'I want you, Venetia. I want you and I know you want me too. As long as you are mortal, what we have between us can never be. My hunger would be too great, the danger to you too strong.

'But as an immortal, Venetia . . . as an immortal you will be mine for ever, my equal, my ageless, undying lover.' He smoothed his hands down her back, her backside, almost as though he believed that through his caresses he might possess her very soul.

'Stay with me, Venetia. One kiss . . . one kiss upon your perfect, white throat and life and death will have no more meaning. Only our passion will exist – for ever.'

She returned his kisses with a fervour which astonished her. Could he feel how much she wanted him, how much she longed to accept the golden cage he was offering to her?

'Oh, Esteban . . . please . . .'

As though he knew that he was losing her, he clutched her more tightly to him, his swollen penis darting its own caresses at the base of her belly.

'For seven hundred years I have hidden from the world, Venetia. Seven hundred years I have suppressed the passion that is within me; for I have never met a woman who excited me as you excite me. Be with me. Be with me for ever . . .'

It was the hardest thing she had ever done; the hardest by far that she would ever do. But with a last kiss she prised his fingers from her flesh and got to her feet, praying he could not see the tears glistening in her blue eyes.

'I am truly free, Esteban? Free to go?'

'You have my word.'

Their fingers met and touched once more, and once more only. The power of that touch, the passion, the electric sensuality, were so great that for a moment she thought of turning back, of baring her throat to his kisses and begging for the gift of immortality. Temptation burned within her. The temptation to share the hunger of perfect passion for ever, and never die . . .

But life was calling her. Ordinary, imperfect life with its disappointments and its pleasures and its uncertainties. Life, which might be flawed and brief, but which could never become a cage as Esteban's existence had become; not even a cage of purest gold.

'Goodbye, Esteban. I will never forget you.'

Her heart breaking and her body yearning for Esteban's caresses, she turned and walked away across the soft, dew-fresh grass.

Towards the dawn.

Already published

BACK IN CHARGE
Mariah Greene

A woman in control. Sexy, successful, sure of herself and of what she wants, Andrea King is an ambitious account handler in a top advertising agency. Life seems sweet, as she heads for promotion and enjoys the attentions of her virile young boyfriend.

But strange things are afoot at the agency. A shake-up is ordered, with the key job of Creative Director in the balance. Andrea has her rivals for the post, but when the chance of winning a major new account presents itself, she will go to any lengths to please her client – and herself . . .

0 7515 1276 1

THE DISCIPLINE OF PEARLS
Susan Swann

A mysterious gift, handed to her by a dark and arrogant stranger. Who was he? How did he know so much about her? How did he know her life was crying out for something different? Something . . . exciting, erotic?

The pearl pendant, and the accompanying card bearing an unknown telephone number, propel Marika into a world of uninhibited sexuality, filled with the promise of a desire she had never thought possible. The Discipline of Pearls . . . an exclusive society that speaks to the very core of her sexual being, bringing with it calls to ecstasies she is powerless to ignore, unwilling to resist . . .

0 7515 1277 X

HOTEL APHRODISIA
Dorothy Starr

The luxury hotel of Bouvier Manor nestles near a spring whose mineral water is reputed to have powerful aphrodisiac qualities. Whether this is true of not, Dani Stratton, the hotel's feisty receptionist, finds concentrating on work rather tricky, particularly when the muscularly attractive Mitch is around.

And even as a mysterious consortium threatens to take over the Manor, staff and guests seem quite unable to control their insatiable thirsts . . .

0 7515 1287 7

AROUSING ANNA
Nina Sheridan

Anna had always assumed she was frigid. At least, that's what her husband Paul had always told her – in between telling her to keep still during their weekly fumblings under the covers and playing the field himself during his many business trips.

But one such trip provides the chance that Anna didn't even know she was yearning for. Agreeing to put up a lecturer who is visiting the university where she works, she expects to be host to a dry, elderly academic, and certainly isn't expecting a dashing young Frenchman who immediately speaks to her innermost desires. And, much to her delight and surprise, the vibrant Dominic proves himself able and willing to apply himself to the task of arousing Anna . . .

0 7515 1222 2

PLAYING THE GAME
Selina Seymour

Kate has had enough. No longer is she prepared to pander to the whims of lovers who don't love her; no longer will she cater for their desires while neglecting her own.

But in reaching this decision Kate makes a startling discovery: the potency of her sexual urge, now given free rein through her willingness to play men at their own game. And it is an urge that doesn't go unnoticed – whether at her chauvinistic City firm, at the château of a new French client, or in performing the duties of a high-class call girl . . .

0 7515 1189 7

THE WOMEN'S CLUB
Vanessa Davies

Sybarites is a health club with a difference. Its owner, Julia Marquis, has introduced a full range of services to guarantee complete satisfaction. For after their saunas and facials the exclusively female members can enjoy an 'intimate' massage from one of the club's expert masseurs.

And now, with the arrival of Grant Delaney, it seems the privileged clientele of the women's club will be getting even better value for their money. This talented masseur can fulfil any woman's erotic dreams.

Except Julia's . . .

0 7515 1343 1

SATURNALIA
Zara Devereux

Recently widowed, Heather Logan is concerned about her sex-life. Even when married it was plainly unsatisfactory, and now the prospects for sexual fulfilment look decidedly thin.

After consulting a worldly friend, however, Heather takes his advice and checks in to Tostavyn Grange, a private hotel-cum-therapy centre for sexual inhibition. Heather had been warned about their 'unconventional' methods, but after the preliminary session, in which she is brought to a thunderous climax – her first – she is more than willing to complete the course . . .

0 7515 1342 3

Forthcoming publications

DARES
Roxanne Morgan

It began over lunch. Three different women, best friends, decide to spice up their love-lives with a little extra-curricular sex. Shannon is first, accepting the dare of seducing a motorcycle despatch rider – while riding pillion through the streets of London.

The others follow, Nadia and Corey, hesitant at first but soon willing to risk all in the pursuit of new experiences and the heady thrill of trying to out-do each other's increasingly outrageous dares . . .

0 7515 1341 5

SHOPPING AROUND
Mariah Greene

For Karen Taylor, special promotions manager in an upmarket Chelsea department store, choice of product is a luxury she enjoys just as much as her customers.

Richard – virile and vain; Alan – mature and cabinet-minister-sexy; and Maxwell, the androgynous boy supermodel who's fronting her latest campaign. Sooner or later, Karen's going to have to decide between these and others. But when you're shopping around, sampling the goods is half the fun . . .

0 7515 1459 4

[ ]	Back in Charge	Mariah Greene	£4.99
[ ]	The Discipline of Pearls	Susan Swann	£4.99
[ ]	Hotel Aphrodisia	Dorothy Starr	£4.99
[ ]	Arousing Anna	Nina Sheridan	£4.99
[ ]	Playing the Game	Selina Seymour	£4.99
[ ]	The Women's Club	Vanessa Davies	£4.99
[ ]	Saturnalia	Zara Devereux	£4.99

X Libris offers an eXciting range of quality titles which can be ordered from the following address:

Little, Brown and Company (UK),
P.O. Box 11,
Falmouth,
Cornwall TR10 9EN

Alternatively you may fax your order to the above address.
FAX No. 0326 376423.

Payments can be made as follows: cheque, postal order (payable to Little, Brown and Company) or by credit cards, Visa/Access. Do not send cash or currency. UK customers and B.F.P.O. please allow £1.00 for postage and packing for the first book, plus 50p for the second book, plus 30p for each additional book up to a maximum charge of £3.00 (7 books plus).

Overseas customers including Ireland please allow £2.00 for the first book plus £1.00 for the second book, plus 50p for each additional book.

NAME (Block Letters) _____

_____

ADDRESS _____

_____

_____

☐ I enclose my remittance for _____

☐ I wish to pay by Access/Visa card

Number _____

Card Expiry Date _____